BABYLON

BABYLON

Yasmina Reza

Translated by Linda Asher

Seven Stories Press
New York • Oakland • London

This work received support from the French Ministry of Foreign Affairs and the Cultural Services of the French Embassy in the United States through their publishing assistance program.

Seven Stories Press
140 Watt Street
New York, NY 10013
www.sevenstories.com

Library of Congress Cataloging-in-Publication Data

Names: Reza, Yasmina. | Asher, Linda translator.
Title: Babylon / Yasmina Reza ; translated by Linda Asher.
Other titles: Babylone. English
Description: Seven Stories Press first edition. | New York, NY : Seven Stories Press, 2018.
Identifiers: LCCN 2018003838 | ISBN 9781609808327 (hardcover)
Subjects: LCSH: Murder--Investigation--Fiction. | GSAFD: Suspense fiction
Classification: LCC PQ2678.E955 B3313 2018 | DDC 843/.914--dc23
LC record available at https://lccn.loc.gov/2018003838

Book design by Jon Gilbert

Printed in the USA.

9 8 7 6 5 4 3 2 1

for Didier Martiny

"The world isn't tidy; it's a mess.
I don't try to make it neat."

—GARRY WINOGRAND

He's against a wall, in the street. Standing there in suit and tie. He has ears that stick out, a frightened glance, short white hair. He's thin, narrow shoulders. He's holding out a magazine with the word AWAKE on it. The photo caption reads *"Jehovah's Witness—Los Angeles."* The picture dates from 1955. He looked like a little boy.

He's been dead a long time. He was properly dressed for handing out religious tracts. He was alone, driven by a sad, sullen perseverance. At his feet there seems to be a briefcase—the handle shows—that holds dozens more copies that nobody, or hardly anybody, will take from him. And those tracts, in huge printings, recall death as well. The spurts of optimism—too many glasses, too many chairs—that drive us to accumulate things and soon turn them futile. Things and our efforts. The wall he's standing against is massive. You sense that from its heavy opaqueness, from the size of the stone blocks. It is probably still standing, there in Los Angeles. The rest has gone scattered somewhere: the little man in a loose suit with his pointed ears who's set up in front of it to hand out a religious magazine, his white shirt and his dark tie, his trousers worn thin at the knees, his brief-case, his magazines. What does it matter what a person is, thinks, becomes? You're somewhere in the landscape until the day you're not anymore. Yesterday it was raining. I picked up Robert Frank's *The Americans*, it had got lost in the bookcase, stuck at the back of a shelf. I reopened the book I hadn't opened for forty years. I remembered the fellow standing on a street selling a magazine. The photo is grainier, paler than I thought. I wanted to see it again, *The Americans*, the saddest book on earth. Dead people, gas pumps, people alone in cowboy hats. Turning the pages you see a parade of jukeboxes, television sets, trappings of the new prosperity. They're just as alone as the man, these oversized new objects, too heavy, too bright, set down in spots unprepared for them. One fine day someone carries them off. They'll make another little journey, jostled along to the dump. You're somewhere in the landscape until the day you're not. I thought of the

Scopitone jukebox in the harbor at Dieppe. We took off in the little Renault 2CV at three in the morning to go and see the sea. I must have been no more than seventeen and I was in love with Joseph Denner. We barreled along, seven of us, in the jalopy with its belly dragging on the road. I was the only girl. Denner was driving. We headed toward Dieppe drinking from a bottle of Red Valstar. We got to the port at six, we went into the first tavern we saw and got some Picon beer. There was a Scopitone in the place. We cracked up watching the performers. At one point Denner put on Fernand Raynaud, "The Butcher," and we laughed till we cried, from the show and from the Picon.

Then we drove back. We were young. We didn't know it was irretrievable. Today I'm sixty-two years old. I can't say I've figured out how to be happy in life, I couldn't give myself a score of fourteen out of twenty when I come to die, like that colleague of Pierre's who said "Well— maybe fourteen out of twenty," I'd give myself maybe a twelve, because less would look ungrateful or hurt someone, I'd cheat and say twelve out of twenty. When I'm in the ground what difference will it make? Nobody will care whether or not I managed to be happy in life, and I won't much care either.

On my sixtieth birthday, Jean-Lino Manoscrivi invited me to the racetrack at Auteuil. We ran into each other in the stairwell, we were both going up on foot, I to keep a presentable figure, he out of a phobia for enclosed spaces. He was skinny, not tall, a pockmarked face, a high forehead stretching back to the balding man's usual comb-over. He wore glasses with thick frames that made him look old. He lived on the fifth floor, I on the fourth. It made for a kind of complicity, these encounters in the enclosed stairwell no one else ever used. In some modern-day apartment buildings, the stairs are set off and ugly, only used by moving men. In fact the tenants call it the service staircase. For a while, he and I weren't really acquainted, I just knew he worked in appliances; he knew I worked at the Pasteur Institute. My job title—patent engineer—means nothing to people and I no longer try to describe it in any appealing way. Once, Pierre and I had gone upstairs to have a drink at their place, as couples. His wife was some sort of New Age therapist who used to manage a shoe store. They were recently married—I mean, compared to us. Running into Jean-Lino in the stairwell the night before my birthday, I had said, "I'm turning sixty tomorrow." I was dragging my feet and it just came to me like that. "You're not sixty yet, are you, Jean-Lino?" "Soon," he answered. I could see that he wanted to say something nice but he didn't dare. As we got to my floor I added, "It's all over for me, I give up." He asked if I'd ever been to the races. I said no. Stammering a little, he suggested that if I was free, maybe I might join him the next day at Auteuil at lunchtime. When I got to the track he was settled in the restaurant, pressed against the glass wall over the paddock. On the table, a bottle of champagne in a bucket, the turf papers spread out all marked up, peanut shells scattered among old ticket stubs. He was waiting for me like a relaxed fellow hosting friends at his club, in total contrast to the way I knew him. We snacked on some rich dish he chose. He got excited over each race, jumping up, roaring, brandishing his fork with its dangling strands of poached leek. Every five minutes he would go out to smoke half a cigarette and come back in with new strategies. I'd never seen him with that level of energy, and certainly not of happiness. We placed some minor bets on horses whose potential we knew nothing about, he had "a hunch" about them, his private convictions. He won a little bit, maybe the price of the champagne (we'd drunk the whole bottle, mostly he). I pocketed three euros. Three euros, I said to myself, on the day you turned sixty—nice. I sensed that Jean-Lino Manoscrivi was lonely. A Robert Frank character for our times. With his Bic pen and his racing journal, and especially with his fedora. He had put together a little ritual for himself, he'd carved out a space in time that suited him. At the racetrack he took on broader shoulders, even his voice changed.

I thought about my father's sixtieth birthday. We went to eat choucroute at République. That was the age for parents—an enormous, abstract age. Now you're the one who's that age. How can that be? A girl cuts up a little, trots through life in spike heels and face paint, and suddenly she's sixty. I would go off to take pictures with Joseph Denner. He liked photography and I liked everything he liked. I cut my biology classes. Nobody worried about the future in those years. An uncle had given me a secondhand Konika, real professional-looking, all the more since I'd picked up a Nikon strap. Denner had an Olympus that wasn't reflex, we'd focus with a built-in rangefinder. The idea was we would both shoot the same subject at the same instant from the same position and then each make our own image. We'd shoot the street like the greats we admired—passersby and animals at the zoo across from school, but mainly inside the bars Denner was fond of around the Cardinet Bridge. The drifters, the barflies mummified in the cubicles in back. We would develop the contact sheets at some friend's place. We'd compare them and pick the good ones to blow up. What was the "good" one—the best composed? the one that caught some tiny unfathomable interaction? Who can say? I think about Joseph Denner regularly. Sometimes I wonder how he would have turned out. But a guy who dies of cirrhosis of the liver at thirty-six, how could he turn out? Since this thing happened here, it's as if he's been invited back into my head. The whole business would have really made him laugh. *The Americans* gave me back some images of being young. We daydreamed and did nothing. We'd watch people go by, we'd make up lives for them, decide what objects they looked like—a mallet, a bandage . . . We'd laugh. Underneath the laughter there was a slightly bitter boredom. I'd really like to see them again, those pictures we took around the Cardinet Bridge. They probably got thrown out here one day with old papers. After that birthday at Auteuil, I developed some affection for Jean-Lino Manoscrivi. If we left the building at the same time we'd walk a little ways together and sometimes we'd have a coffee at the corner. Outdoors he could smoke, at home not. I saw him as a very gentle man, and I still see him that way. There was never any familiarity between us and we always used the formal *vous*. But we did talk, we sometimes told each other things we didn't tell other people. He especially, but it could happen that I did too. We discovered we had the same dislike for our childhoods, the same desire to just cross them out. One day, speaking of the course of his life journey, he said, "Well anyhow, the worst is over with." I agreed. Jean-Lino was the grandson of Italian Jewish immigrants on his father's side. His father had started out doing odd jobs in a trimmings workshop. He went on to specialize in ribbons, to the point of opening a notions shop during the sixties. A little alleyway storefront on

Avenue Parmentier. His mother tended the register. They lived in a courtyard flat a few steps from the shop. The parents worked hard and were not affectionate; Jean-Lino didn't expand on the topic. He had a brother, much older, who did well in the garment industry. He himself got into trouble, his mother threw him out of the house. He went into the food line after getting a certificate in pastry making. At the most hopeful period in his life, he set up a restaurant. It was hard—no vacations, too little business. In the end, the government employment center paid for his training in mass marketing and a placement agency got him into the Guli stores where he handled after-sales support on home appliances. He'd never had a child. That was the one reproach he dared to level at the fates that ruled his existence. His first wife had left him after the restaurant failed. When he met Lydie, she was already a grandmother by a daughter from an earlier marriage. For the past two years the child had been coming regularly to their apartment. The parents had separated on such bad terms that Social Services got involved, and they would unload the kid at grandma's place on the slightest excuse. With a tenderness that had never found an outlet (except with his cat), Jean-Lino had welcomed little Rémi with open arms, and tried to get the boy to love him. Is it right to want to make someone love you? Isn't that the kind of project that's always doomed to disaster?

The beginnings were chaotic. Five years old when he arrived—the family had been living in the South—the child made a point of ignoring Jean-Lino completely, and would cry the moment Lydie moved out of sight. He was an ordinary little boy, rather plump, with a nice smile and dimples. The difficulties of taming were made worse by Jean-Lino's cat Eduardo, an unpleasant animal picked up on the streets of Vicenza who could only be spoken to in Italian. Lydie had worked things out with Eduardo. She'd dangle her pendant before him and the cat would follow the swinging rose quartz, mesmerized (the stone had been "a gift" to Lydie somewhere in Brazil). On the other hand, Eduardo had taken against Rémi. He would swell to twice his size whenever the child appeared, and would hiss in a disturbing way. Jean-Lino tried to bring his cat into line with no help from anyone. Lydie had solved the situation by keeping Eduardo in the bathroom. Rémi would go and torment him by imitating his miauling through the door. Jean-Lino tried to stop the boy but he lacked authority. When there was no one near, he would go quietly to soothe the animal through the door by murmuring a few Italian endearments. Rémi refused to call Jean-Lino "Grampa Jean-Lino." Actually, it's wrong to say the boy refused; he simply never did call him Grampa Jean-Lino, despite the man's constant chant of *Grampa Jean-Lino's going to read you a story now,* or *If you eat all your fish, Grampa Jean-Lino will buy you this or that*. Grampa Jean-Lino was simply disdained by Rémi, who did not give a damn about him. When the boy had any reason to use his name at all he called him Jean-Lino, who felt foolishly touched by just the use of his first name uttered with no familial qualifier. As time went on, changing strategy, he got it into his head to win the boy's heart through fun and games. He taught him to say silly things like Howdydoody, which the boy loved and instantly converted to Whodiddoodydoody, then just Youdodoody, chanting it over and over, putting on crazy voices or yelling it right at Jean-Lino, in public if possible and very loud. I was a spectator at this little performance myself in the apartment-house lobby.

Pretending to laugh along, Jean-Lino told the boy, "You know, if you repeat a joke too often it stops being funny." He could no longer cut off the routine. The more he tried to reason with him the more the boy repeated the line. Lydie offered no help, holding with the theory that you reap what you sow. When she sensed a kind of disheartenment in Jean-Lino she would just say, in a sorrowful tone, *Look, leave the poor kid alone, you can't go blaming someone who's a victim of their parents' bad behavior*. In hindsight, I suppose she sensed the dangers in her husband's one-sided attachment.

I should say something about the building lobby. It's a long space, lit in the daytime by the half-window in the entry door. The elevator is in the center facing the door. You get to the stairwell through a side door in a recess on the left. The right-hand corridor leads back to the trashbin area. When the three of them were together, Lydie would take the elevator up with her grandson while Jean-Lino climbed the stairs on foot. When Jean-Lino was alone with Rémi, the boy insisted on the elevator. Getting him into the stairwell meant dragging him there howling. Jean-Lino couldn't take the elevator. Over his lifetime it had grown impossible for him to take airplanes, elevators, the subway and the new trains with their sealed windows. One day, the boy clung to the stairwell gate like a monkey to keep from going in, and Jean-Lino finally sat down on the bottom steps with tears in his eyes. Rémi sat beside him and asked, "Why don't you ever want to take the elevator?"

"Because I'm afraid."

"I'm not afraid, I can do it."

"You're too young to go alone."

After a while, Rémi did climb the stairs, hoisting himself along the banister. Jean-Lino followed along behind.

If I had to pick a single image from among all those that persist in my head, it would be the one of Jean-Lino seated in the half-darkness on the Moroccan chair in our living room, his hands locked onto the armrests in the midst of a jumble of chairs that no longer had any reason to be there. Jean-Lino Manoscrivi petrified on that uncomfortable chair, in the room where the glasses I'd frantically bought for the occasion still lined the buffet, the platters of celery and chips, all the leavings of the party arranged in an optimistic moment. Who can determine the starting point of events? Who knows what murky, and perhaps long-ago, confluence of circumstances governed the business? Jean-Lino had met Lydie Gumbiner in a bar where she was singing. Put that way, we'd imagine a swaying party girl sending a sultry voice through a mike. In fact she was a little creature without much of a bosom, dressed gypsy-style and draped in pendants and charms, who made much of her hairdo, a big orange frizz tamed by decorative barrettes (she wore a charm anklet as well . . .). She was studying jazz with a singing coach, and would occasionally perform in bars (we went to hear her once). She had sung Henri Salvador's "Syracuse" gazing at Jean-Lino who by chance was seated that night at the edge of the stage, mouthing the lyrics along with her: "Before my youth is worn away and my springtimes are over . . ." Jean-Lino was a Salvador fan. They liked each other. He liked her voice. He liked her long gauzy skirts, that taste for the gaudy. He found it appealing that a woman her age had no use for Paris convention. In fact, this was a person who in many regards could not be classified, and who lived her life as if she had certain supernatural abilities. Why did those two beings come together? I had a friend when I was getting my Intellectual Property degree in Strasbourg, a girl who was fairly withdrawn. One day she up and married a gruff, taciturn man. She told me, "He's alone, I'm alone." Thirty years later I ran into her on the train to Brussels, her company was building hot-air balloons for amusement parks, she was still with him and they had three grown children. The end of the story is not so cheerful for the Gumbiner-Manoscrivi couple—but among the infinitely varied arrangements in the world, isn't it often the same pattern? I took some snapshots at our little gathering (I'd called it a "Spring Celebration"). In one picture, Jean-Lino is standing behind Lydie, who's seated on the couch dressed in one of her getups, they're both laughing, faces turned to the left. They're in good form. Jean-Lino looks happy and flushed. He's leaning on the back of the sofa, bent a little over the reddish pouf hairdo. I remember exactly what it was that had made them laugh. The photo was used in the dossier. It caught what any photo catches, a frozen moment never to come again, and which maybe didn't even happen that way at the time. But given that there will never be any later images of Lydie Gumbiner, this one seems to hold some secret meaning, it's suffused with a venomous aura. In some magazine I recently saw a picture of Josef Mengele during the 1970s in Argentina. He is sitting outdoors somewhere, in a polo shirt, in a crowd of notably younger boys and girls. One of the girls is clinging to his arm. She's laughing. The Nazi doctor is laughing. They're both merry and relaxed, a testament to the sunshine and the lightness of life. The photo would hold no interest without the date and the name of the central figure. The caption upends the interpretation. Is that true for all photographs?

—

I don't know how that idea for a Spring Celebration got started in my head. We never did that kind of thing in the house, neither drinks nor celebration, much less for springtime. When we have friends in, it's never more than six people sitting around a table. Early on I'd wanted to do something with girlfriends from the Pasteur, along with a few of Pierre's colleagues, and then I thought of other names, I began to envision some more or less fruitful interactions, and right away the question of chairs came up. Pierre said, "Borrow some chairs from the Manoscrivis upstairs."

"Without inviting them?"

"Yes inviting them. She could even sing!"

The Manoscrivi pair didn't interest Pierre, but if anything he found Lydie more amusing than Jean-Lino. I sent out forty or so invitations. I immediately regretted it. I lay awake the whole night. How was I going to seat all those people? We had seven chairs, counting the Moroccan thing. The Manoscrivis probably had about the same number. The big Moroccan chair was a pest but how could we get it out of the way? Aside from the chairs, the soft hassock and the couch together could, given an ideal synergy-combination, seat another seven people. Three times seven makes twenty-one. Plus a stool from the basement—so all right, twenty-two. (I'd considered the chest as well, but the chest had to serve as another surface along with the coffee table.) We'd need ten more chairs, but folding ones. They'd have to be foldable so they could be unfolded as needed and not stand there open as if they were waiting for spectators, but where would I get folding chairs? The apartment wasn't spacious enough to allow for thirty unfolded chairs, not to mention the icy uniformity of rental chairs. And why would we need so many chairs? When you give that kind of informal buffet supper—yes, informal!!—people don't all sit, they talk standing up, they move around, you have to expect some back-and-forth, random sitting, people perch on chair arms or squat on the floor, relaxed, leaning against the wall, of course! About the glasses . . . I got up in the night to count how many we had. Thirty-five, various kinds. Plus six champagne goblets in another cupboard. In the morning I told Pierre, We have no glasses. Got to buy twenty champagnes and some wine-glasses. Pierre said he'd seen plastic champagne goblets. I said, Ah no, absolutely not, I'm already unhappy having paper plates, the glasses have got to be glass. Pierre said it's stupid to buy goblets we'll never use again. I said,

We're not drinking champagne out of plastic like at some office retirement party! Pierre said, They sell these super-rigid imitation-glass flutes that are just fine. I looked on the Internet and ordered three boxes of ten "Elegance" champagne flutes each and three boxes each holding fifty disposable knives, forks, and spoons in metallized plastic, stainless-steel style. That calmed me down until the Saturday afternoon of the party when I had a new crisis about the glasses. We had champagne goblets but no wineglasses. After wandering around the Deuil-l'Alouette shops, I came home with thirty wineglasses. And a carton of six champagne goblets. I pulled out a never-used tablecloth, laid it on the chest, and set out all the cups, the champagne glasses, the wineglasses, the hybrids, and even four little vodka glasses in case someone wanted vodka. There were more than a hundred glasses counting the ones from the kitchen. Lydie came to the door at six o'clock, already partly done up, with a chair on either arm. We went upstairs to get the others. There was a yellow velvet armchair in the bedroom. I had never seen their bedroom. The same space as ours except ten times as colorful, ten times more bordello-like, icons on the wall, a poster of Nina Simone half-naked in a white string dress, and the bed in a different position. Eduardo the Cat lay among the pillows, mistrustful and languid. "What are you doing there!" Lydie cried. She clapped her hands and the cat took off. She said, "I don't allow him in the bedroom." I saw what looked like a chamber pot with a wooden lid. In a glance I could tell that Jean-Lino had had no say in the interior decoration, not that you could make out his personal touch elsewhere either, but the rest of the apartment had more the feel of the random compromise between lives. The window was half-open, framed in silky panels like a British candy box, floating gently; in the distance over the apartment buildings you could make out a bit of the Eiffel Tower not visible from our flat. Their bedroom seemed gayer, more youthful than ours. Lifting the very heavy armchair, I was jealous of their bedroom. I have often been weighed down by the bedrooms in my life. Childhood room. Hospital rooms. Hotel rooms with a lousy view. It's the window that makes the room. The space it outlines, the light it brings in. And its curtains. Those sheer panels! I've been in the hospital three times in my life, counting childbirth. Each time I've been oppressed by the hospital room with its big, slightly frosted windows showing a symmetrical row of buildings, or lopped branches, or an overexpansive sky. The hospital room drained me of hope each time. Even with the baby nearby in his glass cradle.

One of Robert Frank's best-known photos is a view of Butte, a mining town in Montana, taken from the window of a hotel room. Rooftops, warehouses. Smoke in the distance. Half the landscape is blocked on either side by net curtains. The childhood bedroom I shared with my sister Jeanne looked out partly on the wall of a gymnasium. The stucco was crumbling off in great chunks. If I leaned to the left, I could see a street without people but with a bus stop. We lived in Puteaux in a brick apartment house, since demolished (I've gone by there, I recognize nothing). We had exactly those same curtains, the same weave, the same slightly rumpled broad vertical border. They opened on the same dismal picture of the world. The window ledge was the same too. A ledge in soiled stone, too narrow, supporting nothing. The Butte hotel room looks out on some dreary shacks and an empty highway. The one in Puteaux gave onto a rear wall with no openings. You would never have put that kind of fabric in front of a glorious thing. I told Lydie, "I worry this armchair will be bulky." "Yes, yes, at worst we can take it down later."

She led me into the living room. She had created a little jungle on the balcony, the boxlike kind of terrace they put on modern buildings, the sort you don't go out onto much. There was a big mimosa spreading its branches that you could see from below.

Potted shrubs were budding. Sometimes the water she poured on them would splash down onto our terrace. I said, "It's wonderful, your balcony." She showed me her sprouting tulips and some crocuses that had bloomed that very morning. "You need anything else? Plates, glasses?"

"I think I have enough."

"While you're here, could you sign a petition against grinding up baby chicks?"

"They grind up baby chicks?"

"The males. They can't become hens so they're chopped up alive in the grinding machines."

"How horrible!" I said as I added my name and signature to a list.

"Napkins? I have these napkins in a crumpled linen that don't need ironing."

"I have everything I need."

"Jean-Lino went down to buy some champagne. And to smoke his little Chesterfield."

"You shouldn't have."

"Please."

She was much more excited than I was. My anxiety attacks had exhausted me and the party loomed like a punishment. Her pleasure made me ashamed. I found her touching and sweet. She hadn't expected this invitation from neighbors she saw as condescending. We left the flat with three more chairs. Downstairs I said, "This is perfect, thanks so much, Lydie, now let's go make ourselves beautiful!"

She gripped my wrist in a show of complicity. "One of these days I'll have to do a readjustment on your aura."

"What does that mean?"

"I'll check you out with my crystal. Clear whatever's clogged, cleanse the organs. Restore the flow."

"That'll take years."

She laughed and disappeared into the stairwell, shaking her orange hairdo.

⁓

More on the curtains: my friend in early adolescence (before my Denner years) was named Joelle. She was beautiful and funny. We were never an inch apart, day or night. Her family was even crazier than mine. Among all kinds of nutty stuff we used to do oil paintings—I still have a few of them, overloaded with gunk—we wrote songs, stories, we lived in Pataugas boots and boys' sweaters, it was the beatnik period. Myself, I never did more than grass and a little alcohol, Joelle got into acid and other freak-out things, and our friendship began to fall apart. One year she came back from Asia by air ambulance, she had taken some hallucinogenic mushroom that unhinged her. She'd just turned eighteen. Twenty years later she telephoned me. She'd found me through my sister on Facebook. I went to see her in Aubervilliers, in a flat that looked out on an interior courtyard. Joelle was just back from the Antilles with a child by a Martiniquais guy who took off into the bush. She had gotten a nursing certificate, she was looking for work. They were living in two connected rooms, an entry hall with a table in it and a bedroom. Dark rooms, made still darker by faded curtains. While it was still late daytime Joelle lit a lamp. We sat talking in that mixture of daylight and electric light that brings back the oppressive atmosphere of Sundays. Sunday was the only day in our house when we could relax about saving electricity, normally we had to turn out the lights in a room even before we left it. Jeanne and I had got used to living in darkness, I much preferred an un-sad darkness to this lugubrious combination. Joelle made me tea, I watched her sitting there with her anxious little boy against the yellowish background. I thought, *We're not going to get anywhere.* I left at the end of the afternoon, abandoning her for the second time in my life.

~

An hour before the party things were pretty much under control, the platters filled, the quiches ready for the oven. Pierre would take care of the salads. On the clothing front, two outfits had been set out for a few days now in the full understanding that in the end I would wind up putting on the no-problem no-risk black dress. I swallowed a Xanax and went to pretty up with a new anti-aging product prescribed by Gwyneth Paltrow. Intellectually I disapprove of the term "anti-aging," which I find guilt-inducing and dumb, but another part of my brain buys into the therapeutic terminology. I recently ordered

Cate Blanchett's favorite cream over the Internet, on the claim that every stylish Australian carried it in her purse. There must be something a little wrong with me. On the radio people talked about the psychological fatigue of the French people. Despite the vagueness of the idea, I was pleased to learn that the French were in the same condition I am. The French had definitely lost their sense of safety. The same old song again. Who can call themselves safe? Everything's uncertain. It's the basic condition of life. On top of that, over the air they were saying people are alarmed about the weakening of the social bond. Neo-liberalism and globalization—those two calamities—are apparently obstructing the creation of bonds. I thought to myself, You're creating a social bond tonight in your apartment in Deuil-l'Alouette. You're lighting candles, you're plumping cushions for your guests, you put the onion tarts in the fridge and you're applying your face cream with circular upward motions as prescribed. You're giving a little touch of youth to existence. A woman is supposed to be cheerful. Unlike a man, who is entitled to spleen and melancholy. After a certain age a woman is condemned to good spirits. When you sulk at twenty it's sexy, when you do it at sixty it's a drag. They didn't say "create a social bond" when I was young, I don't know when that phrase—in the singular—dates from. Nor what it means: the bond reduced to its abstract form has no virtue in itself. Another one of those hollow expressions.

My mother died ten days ago. I didn't see a lot of her, the death doesn't change much in my life except that somewhere on earth there used to exist *my mother*. Yesterday I had a visit from the home health aide who had taken care of her through the last period, and whom I owed money. A huge woman who always scared me and who pants when she talks. She had heard about the drama in our building and was obviously hungry for the details. Disappointed at my reticence, and all the while munching on a St Michel cookie, she switched to the story of a woman baker in Vitrolles who had killed her children on Christmas Eve. In the nighttime she had wrapped the gifts, set them beneath the tree, then went into her son's room and pressed the pillow over his face till he smothered. Then she went to the daughter's room and did exactly the same thing. The aide said, "She wraps the presents, puts them under the tree, and she goes right upstairs and kills the kids." She said, "What I don't like is, they tell you all that and then afterward it's total silence. You hear the story over all the radio stations and then zero. They lure you in and then they slam the door in your face. The wars, the massacres, all that's too global," she said, picking up another cookie. "To me, the global stuff, that doesn't do much for me. It doesn't take me out of myself. A story from regular life, yes. It fills out the day. People talk about it. You don't think about your own problems anymore. I'm not saying it's consoling, but in a way yes. Like, why did she put the presents under the tree, in your opinion? I got along real well with your momma, she was so nice that lady!"

"Yes, yes."

"A nice lady. And nice with everybody."

"I should let you go, Madame Anicé, I've got a job to finish ..."

She rearranged the waistline of her T-shirt, whose print reminded me of the Formica countertop patterns from the 1960s, and slowly got to her feet. "I've got a theory on the Christmas presents ..." In Ginette Anicé's physical person, just two elements reveal an interest in self-presentation: earrings—two gold studs of the sort used to cover the puncture, and the spit curls along her forehead. Her hair is short all over except for some length at the forehead, inch-long extensions, enough to allow the fingers to shape little ringlets ... They're barely noticeable, it takes someone like me who's alert to hairdos to see them. They run along the top rim of the forehead at regular intervals, but make no mistake, they're not just some natural curly border, this is bangs worked into separate locks, with decorative intent; they're actual *spit curls*.

"My theory," said Ginette, "is that it just hit her while she was busy doing the presents. It was life-fatigue that hit her."

"That could be ..."

She picked up her felt coat.

"Madame Anicé, would you like to have a crocheted pillow cover?"

"Ah, those covers your momma used to make . . . That's kind but I don't have any cushions at home."

"Or maybe a doily for the back of the chair?"

"A doily, as a keepsake—sure! . . . And that there, that's the picture that was in your momma's bedroom!"

It annoyed me that she kept saying "your *momma*." I can't stand those infantilizing expressions. She was talking about a picture of (our son) Emmanuel at La Seyne-sur-Mer. My mother kept that photo in a frame on her night table. A picture of her grandson at twelve, in a bathing suit with a sun hat. She also had an old birthday picture of Jeanne's children. I always wondered what those pictures meant to her, I mean emotionally. In my view, she didn't see them, those frames were set beside her bed by convention. We live under the rule of convention. We run on rails. Before she left, Ginette Anicé announced that she had quit the health agency and only wanted to work private home-care jobs. So actually she was unemployed. I said I would ask around, when in fact I would never recommend her to anyone. I closed the door behind her and looked at the photo. I looked at Emmanuel's little body. His skinny arms. He was the busiest child on the beach. Always with a bucket in hand, carrying it empty or full, going from the water to the brush at the end of the sand to build who knows what miniature world, back and forth dozens of times, looking for stones, chunks of wood, shells, all kinds of creatures in the foam. When he went into the water, it was never to swim. Standing in the water up to his waist, he would say, "Momma, tell me who you want to see die?" I would say the name of one of his teachers at school (that was the game).

"OK, yes—Monsieur Vivaret! . . . *What are you doing there, Emmanuel?!*" Pcch pcch! Pcch!!

And he'd splash into the waves with huge leaps.

"Madame Pellouze!" I'd say.

"Emmanuel, will you put down that Kalachnikov!! . . ." Splash splash pchhh bang bang!

"Madame Farrugia!"

We'd kill them all off one by one.

These days you're a "Content Champion" for an ad agency. When people ask what you do, you say Project Chief/Editorial Consultant (the English title is so much nicer!). The photograph gives me back your body from before. I had stopped thinking about it. I never open the albums I used to put together. Those thin arms—I'd like to feel them circling my neck again. Me too, I don't care about the global stuff either, she's right, that Anicé.

～

One day, with no warning, Rémi put his arm around Jean-Lino Manoscrivi's neck.

It happened one Sunday at the Hippopotamus. The three of them were having lunch with a couple of friends from Lydie's jazz club. Rémi, who was bored the way all kids are at the table, had asked permission to go blow bubbles on the open veranda. Jean-Lino was keeping an eye on him when suddenly there was no more Rémi. Jean-Lino goes to see.

No Rémi. He runs down the steps, looks up and down the Avenue General Leclerc:

Nothing. He goes back inside, looks upstairs. No one. Grandma Lydie is frantic. Jean-Lino and she go back outside. They rush to the right, to the left, spin about, run back into the Hippopotamus, question the waiters, run out again. They shout the child's name, the cityscape is empty, wide open to the winds. The jazz friends have stayed at the table, petrified, no longer touching their plates. A nearby couple discreetly tilt their chins toward a sideboard with a kind of potted palm alongside. Lydie's girlfriend finally understands the signals, she gets up and finds Rémi crouching behind the flower tub, giggling over his prank. The desperate Manoscrivis return. Lydie flings herself on the child and hugs him to her. She all but congratulates him on his reappearance. Order returns. Jean-Lino hasn't said a word. He has sat down, pale and somber. Rémi too is back in his seat. They offer him an *île flottante* for dessert. He rocks on his chair like a smug kid and then, nobody knows why, he stands up, goes and puts his arms around Jean-Lino, and lays his head on the man's shoulders. Jean-Lino's heart swells beyond reason. He believed in the secret triumph of love, like all rejected lovers whose fever flares up anew at the slightest unexpected gesture. Those same gestures mean nothing coming from a person who's already been won over. I could write plenty on the topic. The guy who never gave you a glance and then one day just randomly, out of inadvertence or perversity, shoots you an unexpected signal—I know what that can set off.

~

I should find out how Jean-Lino's aunt is doing. The visit from Ginette Anicé made me think of her. Jean-Lino had brought his father's sister to France and got her placed in a Jewish retirement home. I had visited there with him one afternoon. We went to the cafeteria, a large lobby converted to an entirely functional space—floor in patterned tiles, glossy walls, people in wheelchairs seated at tables with visitors. You would have thought that all the materials in the place had been chosen for their high capacity for echo and resonance. The aunt charged ahead with her walker. Quick wit, lively legs. The body, and especially the head, shaken by constant uncontrolled movements that seemed not to bother her but that made her speech muffled and halting. And at the same time, she spoke three languages: a disciplined, old-fashioned

French, now half-forgotten; Italian; and Ladin, a dialect of the Dolomite mountains. Jean-Lino settled us at a rear table, in front of a television set tuned at top volume to a channel running short films. During the conversation (if you can call it that), Jean Lino plucked hairs from her face with his fingers. Does she know what's happened to her nephew? Who does she ever talk to, with her bobbing head, in the wilderness of that hall? The slightest thing can make me doubt the coherence of the world. Its laws seem all independent of one another and they clash. In my little closet of an office at the Pasteur, a fly is exasperating me. I can't stand it when a fly is stupid. I open the window wide and, instead of heading out into the trees around our building, it comes zigzagging back into the room and toward the far wall. Two seconds ago it was beating against the windowpane, flapping every whichway to get out, and now that the air is flowing in and the sky is spreading its welcoming arms, the damn thing is back indoors wandering crazily about in the shadows. It would serve the bug right if I shut it in and washed my hands of it. But it has that odious buzz going for it. In fact I wonder if that buzz wasn't created just to protect flies, keep people from imprisoning them. If it weren't for that performance I'd be merciless. I grab my big patent-law book and chase the fly toward the window, I mean I try to, but instead of surrendering to the merciful weapon it swerves, keeps just out of reach, and goes up to cling to the ceiling molding. Why do I have to put up with such a waste of time? The aunt used to live in the mountains. She still talked about her chickens, the chickens would come into the house and perch everywhere. She wanted to go back to her village to see the yearly cattle-drive up into the hills, she wanted to hear the clang of the cow-bells. I'm going to phone the rest home.

When the lawyer asked me what Jean-Lino was to me, I said a friend. The man acted as if he didn't understand the word. He wanted to know what I meant by it. One evening, early in our friendship—the term is absolutely precise—I was coming home from the office a little late. Jean-Lino was outside with his Chesterfield cigarettes, his neck naked to the wind. And every time, that smile when he would catch sight of me, the yellowed teeth and their overbite, dazzling in its way. He was cinched into a juvenile-looking fake-leather motorcycle jacket I'd never seen on him. I said, "That's new? Where's the Harley?"

"Zara. On sale."

"Bravo."

"You like it? It's not a little tight?"

I put an arm around him, laughing, and I said, "I adore you for buying that!" He laughed too. He said the sales-girl had complimented him. He was dying of heat in the fitting room, he couldn't stay in there longer than ten seconds. I told him there had rarely been a piece of clothing so ill-suited to its owner.

"Oh really? Shit!"

The two of us laughed hard there under the streetlamp, him coughing his lungs out. He wiped his eyes behind the thick-framed glasses. His pitted face shone a little, I'd never asked him where that scarring came from. I went inside first. He wanted to stay out a bit longer, get some air—translation: have a last smoke. Turning back at the lobby door, through the glass I saw him walking a little in the parking area, his body stooped in his new biker jacket, one hand pressing his hair down along the sides, that look of delight entirely gone now, the way he probably was just before I turned up. I told myself, That's where we're at now—you're growing older too, just like everyone you know, and I felt how I belonged to that throng moving along, hand in hand, growing old, moving along toward something unknown.

What matters, looking at a photo, is the photographer behind it. Not so much the person who pressed the shutter as the one who's chosen the picture, who said, "This one I keep, this one I'll show." To a hurried eye there was nothing special about the picture of the Jehovah's Witness. Not the subject, not the lighting. A tired guy in a business suit and tie peddling a magazine. The classic nobody figure you place in the background on a sidewalk in a film on the 1950s. Among the hundreds of photos Robert Frank must have taken in the course of his trip across America, and among those he ultimately selected, there's this one. At its center is a white patch, the offered magazine, the wrist turned out to show the title, AWAKE, a word completely at odds with the funereal look of its bearer. But it would be wrong to think that the photograph was chosen for its ironical aspect. I hadn't recalled the title, myself; what I remembered was the unease of the mouth, or of the eyes, I remembered something that's not there: the sense of a day of weak sunlight. He could be selling strawberries or daffodils with the same obstinacy, frail inside his suit, swallowed up by that wall erected for a conquering human force. You wonder where he goes at night. You know that at some point there must have been some bad bifurcation.

⌇

I lost my mother a week ago. I was there. She raised one shoulder, as if something was bothering her, and then nothing more happened. I called to her. I called several times. And there was nothing more. My friend Lambert told me that his mother had asked him recently, "How old are you?"

"Seventy, Momma."

"Seventy years old!" his mother exclaimed. "You deserve to be an orphan by now, my boy!"

Jeanne and I emptied the apartment last weekend. Two tiny rooms at Boulogne-Billancourt. A free cleanout service came to take away the furniture and the kitchen equipment. And all the objects—wooden pig, plaster cat, candlesticks, the Provençal doll, glass paperweights, bud vases—that we tossed into the trash bags. In fact, almost everything, except for the contents of a few drawers and the clothing. And the mushroom-shaped nutcracker I made in a high school woodworking shop fifty years ago, found among other knickknacks in a badly battered shoebox from the André shops. I would never have imagined the thing still existed. Jeanne didn't remember it, she refused to believe I'd made it. From a storage sack stuffed in the rear of a closet we pulled crocheted placemats, crocheted pillow covers, the crocheted patchwork afghan spread that used to cover our parents' bed, all of which for some incomprehensible reason we had spared from the truck. Our mother was the champion of crochet. After she retired, she had nothing but that to do. Errands, TV, the needles and hooks in front of the TV. Before she was even walking, Jeanne's daughter was crawling around in crocheted diaper covers and little skirts. What shall we do with these? Jeanne asked.

"We can give them to some charity."

"Who'd want them?"

"We should've dumped them with the rest of the stuff."

"Yes."

"And the clothes too."

"Yes."

The clothing was carefully hung, pressed tight into a narrow wardrobe. Till the very end, even totally bed-ridden, she insisted on being *presentable*. She would say, "I'm afraid they'll find me dead and dirty." The dirty old lady, that's what I dread. We pulled out blouses, cardigans, the winter coat. We laid them on a three-level step stool, the single leftover from the stripped house. We knew it all by heart. We'd seen it all for years. Outfits out of fashion, out of season. The wardrobe of an ordinary woman who lives quietly, goes off to work, comes home from work, keeps a proper household, never even conceived of committing the least friskiness, not in appearance or perhaps in anything else—but as to that, who can say. Jeanne and I knew every item in the armoire since almost forever, she was wearing them already back in Puteaux, the same rough woolens, the same matching sets, mostly deep green trimmed in beige, the polyester bathrobe less aged but still seen for years.

Nicely folded in a corner there were the silk scarves we'd given her when scarves were in fashion, we'd kept giving her new ones in pleasing colors, without noticing that she never wore the earlier ones. They were wrapped in tissue-paper dustcovers. Jeanne took one and wrapped it around her head, meaning to do her Audrey Hepburn.

I said, "So when does Ramadan start?" We laughed and a weird kind of sorrow rose in my throat in that tiny empty flat where just about nothing was left of an entire life. Fat Anicé had felt obliged to accept the doily. She'd said, "As a keepsake, sure," with the gesture of a good girl doing a service. She could have pretended to be touched or to admire the work, but no, she stuck it into the bottom of her bag like a meaningless thing. I'm mad at myself for giving it to her. A woman crochets her whole life long and leaves some bits of craft that are no use to anyone. She would invent patterns but nobody cared. Who's interested in crochet patterns? Death carries everything off, and that's good. Got to make room for the newcomers. In our family we carried this to extremes. The biblical model—this father begat that one who begat etcetera—not in our house. On neither side. I knew none of my grandparents except for my father's mother, the widow of a railroad man, a woman who loved nothing but the birds she overfed on her windowsills.

The apartment upstairs is still sealed. The yellow tape and the two wax seals are still on the door. From time to time I go up, on purpose to see. What happened here has gradually wafted away, the air is as it was before, I lean out over the railing of my balcony and there's nothing but the ordinary scene: the privet hedges, the shrubs in their basins, the cars parked between the freshly painted lines. I used to see the Manoscrivis go by in that parking area. I would see them climb into the Laguna station wagon, she always at the wheel when they were together. He would finish his cigarette before getting in, she had time to back out of the space.

Eighteen people came. I had prepared for twice that many. Pals from forever, some colleagues of Pierre's, Jeanne and her ex-husband, my niece, the Manoscrivis, my girlfriends from Pasteur or from Font-Pouvreau with or without boyfriends, and also, though he didn't stay long, Emmanuel. No sooner did Jeanne arrive, carrying a homemade orange cake as if she were bringing a tub of caviar, than she rushed into the kitchen to wrap the cake in a towel and shove it hard into the fridge. I saw immediately that she was in one of those elated moods that exhaust me. My sister has completely unstable mood swings. She can change from one hour to the next, even less. The bad mood is radical, a state of gloom, almost silent and somewhat pleasant. But the good mood is worse. She sings under her breath, a show of good cheer with girlish flourishes and determinedly silly inflections. She was beginning a secret affair with a picture-framer.

In the euphoria of the start-up, she had just bought herself an S&M leash and collar. She insisted on drawing me aside to show me the kit on her cellphone. She also wanted to get hold of a small whip, she'd seen a very nice one on the Internet, a knout with four tails on a crocodile handle. But it cost fifty-four euros and the site said "Beware! This object is VERY painful!" I asked to see what the framer looked like but she didn't have a picture of him. He was sixty-four, five years older than she, married, arms thick and muscular from rowing, she said, and tattooed. I thought, So how come no tattooed guy with a whip turns up in my life? I felt finished, out of the game, fit for putting together little suburban parties with family and ultra-conventional folks. I'm irritated with myself for thinking that way. I'm happy with my husband. Pierre is cheerful, easy to live with. Not overtalkative—I don't go for talkative. He is at my disposition without being a pushover or submissive. He's loving. I like his skin. We know each other inside out. I object to his too-unconditional love. He doesn't put me in danger. He doesn't magnify me. He loves me even when I look bad, which is not at all reassuring. There's no electricity between us; was there ever? What a pitiful inventory! I'm the fir tree in that Hans Christian Andersen story: If only something more alive, more intoxicating, would come along! No matter the forest, the snow, the birds, the hares—the fir tree takes no pleasure in any of all that, all it wants is to grow, to be tall enough to view the world. When it has finally grown tall, it dreams of being cut down and carried off by the loggers to become a ship's mast and travel the seas; when its branches have grown out full enough, it dreams of being cut down and carried off to become a Christmas tree. The fir tree languishes, dying of desire. In the heated parlor, as it is being trimmed and decorated, hung with garlands of sweets, a star set on its top, it dreams of evening-time and candles on its branches, it dreams that the entire forest will come to press against the windowpanes in envy. Later, alone in the attic, stripped naked, its needles dropping off in the dry winter chill, it takes heart in looking forward to the return of springtime and the outdoors. When it is out in the courtyard, sprawling withered among fresh sprouting flowers, it longs for its old dark attic corner. When the hatchet and the match come along, it thinks of the old summer days, back in the forest.

The Manoscrivis were the first to arrive, at the same time as Nasser and Claudette El Ouardi. A brilliant, austere couple. I knew Nasser from Font-Pouvreau where he was working as an attorney for the EU. He had since set up his own practice in industrial-property law. Claudette is a researcher in bioinformatics. Lydie and Jean-Lino had already introduced themselves at the door as people who'd gone through enormous hardship traveling so far to get to our place. The El Ouardis laughed politely at the joke. The Manoscrivis brought a bottle of champagne and Jean-Lino held a bouquet of small mauve roses with their stems cut very short. Before Jeanne and her ex-husband Serge arrived, we were briefly just the six of us. An absurd void, hesitation, silences, the two couples having settled into opposite ends of the couch, while Pierre and I, half-up and half-down, fussed with drinks or the crudité plates. Jean-Lino was sitting forward on the edge of the cushion, his comb-over firmly plastered to his pate, hands clasped between his spread knees, in a posture of confident expectation. He was wearing a lavender shirt in an American cut, quite elegant I thought, and eyeglasses I didn't recognize—half-round frames the color of sand. Lydie passed around the celery sticks. Not a word took root, no exchange caught on. Silence greeted the end of every sentence. At one point Nasser mentioned Boulevard Brune, and Lydie exclaimed, "Ah, Boulevard Brune, we're doing our next jam session there!"

"Jam?" Nasser said. "What does that mean?"

"Jazz sessions, in public," Lydie answered, smiling broadly.

"Ah, nice . . . very nice. You play an instrument?"

"I sing."

"You sing. Bravo."

Jean-Lino nodded with pride. I added, "She sings very well," and all acquiesced with kindly murmurs. You'd expect some further talk, some minimal curiosity, but no—the conversation fell back into the yawning hole it had risen from. I glanced outside and saw snowflakes. It was snowing! On the first day of spring! "It's snowing!" I cried. I opened the windows. The cold air rushed in. It was snowing. Not little flakes, either—the beautiful heavy flat kind. Everyone rushed out onto the balcony. Claudette and Lydie leaned over the balustrade to see if they melted when they hit the ground. The men said, "It won't last," the women said, "It'll last." People started talking about the climate, the seasons, the I-don't-know-what, everything. Pierre opened a bottle of champagne and the cork shot out among the snowflakes. "Polluter!" Lydie cried. We all laughed as we drank a toast. Pierre told a story about Emmanuel when he was little.

They'd gone off for a week together, father and son, to winter sports in the Alps. They were sharing a room in a hotel that had a sauna in the basement. Coming back up into the room one evening, all relaxed in his robe, Pierre found Emmanuel in tears in front of the TV. "What's wrong?" "It's snowing in Paris!" "Here too, darling, look how pretty it is outside," Pierre said. "The sunset on the mountaintops!" "I want to go back to Deuil-l'Alou-ette!" the boy wailed. He was rolling around on the bed, howling, throwing off whatever his hand fell on, incon-solable at missing the snow in Deuil-l'Alouette. In the end, Pierre threw the remote at him. The thing exploded against the wall, Emmanuel claiming he'd ducked just in time, Pierre always insisting he'd aimed to the side. *"Snow, which is to say, my childhood, which is to say, happiness"*—even though it's not true for me, I always think of that line of Cioran's. Rushing into the kitchen with her cake, Jeanne said, "I nearly broke my neck on your sidewalk!" as if we were responsible for the change in weather. She was wearing some unusual sandals, lashed to her feet with thongs, whose purchase I understood a moment later on seeing her photos of the S&M equipment. Thanks to the snow, the party took off.

People arrived damp and effervescent, in quick sequence. Jeanne's ex-husband Serge (they separated eight years ago, on good terms, and we've all stayed close) appointed himself to door duty, answering the intercom, helping with the coats, improvising introductions. My pal Danielle, who handles documentation at the Pasteur, arrived very upset as well. She had just buried her stepfather that day. At the hospital, when her mother saw the body in its coffin, she had cried, "But Jean-Pierre didn't have a mustache!" The attendant who'd prepared the body had shaved him badly and the shadow beneath the nostrils gave him a Hitler look. When Danielle told that story I remembered the flat tight hairdo, with a harsh part, they'd given my aunt at her funeral—a woman who her whole life had kept up a constant succession of permanent waves and big bouffants. When she was rotting in a retirement home her husband, who to use my mother's expression had never quit "chasing skirts," gave away all her clothes to the Little Sisters of the Poor, except for the outfit she would need to be buried in. "Jean-Pierre didn't have a mustache!" Danielle's mother kept repeating in a frantic tone (Danielle reproduced it perfectly). She apparently went rushing around the room, flinging herself against the walls time and again. In a firmly sane voice Danielle said, "Mama, calm down, we're going to fix it." A man came in, she pointed out the shaving problem, her mother kept saying, "My husband didn't have a mustache!" The man tiptoed back in with a shaving kit. The hairless and powdered Jean-Pierre who emerged bore no greater resemblance to the familiar Jean-Pierre, but her mother leaned into the coffin over the recumbent figure and said, "Oh you are so handsome my darling Pilou!" Later, emerging into the corridor, unsteady and near collapse, she said "You've got to take serious care of me now, Danielle darling, what are you doing tonight? I could cook us a little veal roast, with mushrooms?" Well, girl, Danielle said to herself, so long to partying with your pals, you can't leave your mother all alone tonight. I remarked that I myself had never had a double who called me "girl" and kept me from doing dumb things. "Well, my double does call me 'girl,'" Danielle said, "but I don't listen to her."

"So you did leave her all alone?"

"I handed her over to one of her neighbors, but I've got to have a stiff drink right this minute!"

"You should have brought her along."

"You're insane! Give me a break!" Danielle cried, tossing back a glassful.

From that moment on, Mathieu Crosse, a colleague of Pierre's, started prowling around her. I was in the kitchen slicing a quiche when Emmanuel turned up by surprise, all expansive and beaming like a boy with three parties ahead of him. He seemed astonishingly young among us. He was. The Lallemants arrived with a chicken spice loaf and a book for Pierre from Lambert wrapped in gift paper. Pierre accepted the package gracefully and set it down on a table without unwrapping it. I said, "No, open it! He never opens anything anymore!" It was a first edition of Tartakower's *Breviary of Chess*. A very thoughtful present, because Pierre had been mourning the loss of his boyhood copy. I said, "He never unwraps packages lately, it's a new thing with him." "Am I heading the same way as my father?" Emmanuel said. "I buy clothes and then I don't take them out of the bag and it's a good two weeks before I put them on." "Because you're too young," Pierre said. "You'll see, one day you won't put them on at all." Marie-Jo Lallemant fluffed her wet hair with a kind of sensuous pleasure. "So what are you up to these days, Manu?" I heard her accost Emmanuel, in the tone of someone his own age. She's an orthoptist, and sees herself as a chum to young folks. "Digital marketing," said Emmanuel. "Oh, great!" While I looked for a tray to serve the chicken loaf, I heard phrases like "We set up content sites for B2B companies" and saw Marie-Jo giving complicit nods. "Digital is way more fun than, like, financial planning!" Marie-Jo was totally with him on that.

The Lallemants had just got back from Egypt. Lambert laid out photographs of pyramids with always one or two Asians in the frame, shots of Cairo, storefronts with dummies in them, and then one unusual image. I said, "Oh let's see, let's see that!" It was nothing: a woman viewed from the back walking with a little child. The shot was almost random, not very sharp. I can pull it up today on my computer because Lambert sent it to me online right then (which is why in my album it comes just before the picture of the Manoscrivis laughing). In a street in Cairo, a woman is walking holding the hand of a tiny girl in a long white dress. The street surface there is tiled, probably an esplanade or a broad sidewalk. It's nighttime. All around are men, signs, overlighted shopwindows. The woman is voluminous, her hair concealed by a scarf. It's hard to work out exactly how she's dressed, over a black sweater and dark trousers she's got a knee-length orange tunic. The child comes up to just above her knees, she's all in white except for her bare arms. A kind of priest-like dress with panels, very long, that grazes the ground and must hinder her walking, under that a loose shirt up to the neck. The dress flares out from the waist, the way it would for an adult style, with a notable sweep of fabric. Up top, there's the child's very small head. The nape of the neck is naked except for a tail of braid down the middle, her hair is thin and black, the ears protrude. How old is she? That dress doesn't suit her at all. She's been dolled up and marched out into the night. I immediately identified with that figure in white being launched into years of shame. When I was a child they were always making me *pretty*. I understood that I wasn't naturally pretty. But people shouldn't dress up an unlovely child. She'll feel abnormal. I saw the other children as harmonious. I felt ridiculous in old-lady clothes that kept me from fidgeting, my hair always cut short (throughout my entire childhood my mother forbade me long hair) and pinned back with a barrette to control the curl and bare my forehead. I remember a period when I would do my homework with fake-hair pieces clipped onto my own; I would shake my head regularly to feel them swing and bounce. My mother wanted me to make a good appearance. By which she meant tidy, slicked-back, constrained, and ugly. This woman in the headscarf wasn't thinking of the little girl's well-being. She felt nothing like that in her own body. But mostly, there is no concern for well-being. No one thought of such a thing in our house. I cannot forgive that bitch Anicé for scorning my mother's doily. I can't sleep thinking of it. *She was really nice, your momma!* meaning to please me.

Or to reproach me. My mother was anything but nice. It was impossible to describe her in those terms. On the pretext of death, people strip a person of their essential character. What would have pleased me, instead, would have been for that bitch to take the placemat tenderly, lay it carefully into her bag, treat it at least for the few seconds of farewell as a cherished object. She probably tossed it into the nearest trashcan. I would have done the same, but no one would suspect it. When I wasn't part of a social display, my mother would drag me around like that Cairo mother, preoccupied with other life concerns. When her hands were taken up by the shopping cart, I was supposed to hold onto its side rail. I could trot along for miles with snot running from my nose and my hood askew on my head and she'd never notice. Jeanne and I were always overdressed. Until we were quite old we had to wear hoods for six months of the year. What detail was it that caught my eye when Lambert laid out his inert photographs before us? That pair walking the greenish tile pavement caught me up short. Despite the dispro-portion between the two figures, the overwhelming mother and the child with the pin-like head, you could grasp the whole force of their tiny life. No matter that the photo was taken only a few days before my party, in a different country, a different climate; still it grabbed me and thrust me way back in time. We were ugly, and ill-dressed, my mother and I. We used to go all alone through the streets in that same way, and even though my mother was not large, I felt very small alongside her. Emptying her apartment with Jeanne, I understood how alone she had been throughout her life. When my father had his bouts of madness and hit me, she would turn up in my room to ask me to stop crying. She'd appear on the threshold and say, "All right now, that's enough theater." Then she would go cook dinner and make some dish I liked—a noodle soup, say. In the last months of her life, when we came to visit her, she was possessed by some inexplicable liveliness. Neck straining forward, face at the ready, on the watch for any movement, she was determined not to miss a word exchanged in her presence, and this was despite her deafness. She who all her life had made a specialty of indifference, who had taken a negative counterposition on everything, when it came time to throw in the sponge she was devoured by curiosity.

There's always some millstone character at these things. That evening the millstone was Georges Verbot. He eats, he drinks, he never helps out, and he doesn't talk to anybody. The snow had turned to a soft rain. Plate and glass in hand, Georges Verbot wandered aimlessly among the groups, then went to stare out the window as if to say the scene was at least slightly more interesting outdoors. I was furious that Pierre had invited him again. There's this tendency among many men, I'd noticed, to drag along through their whole lives these annoying millstones whom they find entertaining while nobody else understands why. Way back, Georges was a historian, then he drew comic strips, now he scribbles and just gets by, drinking all the way. He still has a vaguely handsome face that attracts women who have nothing much going on. Catherine Mussin, who still works for Font-Pouvreau, edged over to the window and tried a little opener about the changeable weather. Georges said he liked lousy weather, rain, especially this kind of dismal rain that pisses everyone off. Catherine gave a nervous laugh, charmed by the picturesque. He asked what she did, she said she was a patent engineer, he replied, "Same bullshit as Elisabeth!" She laughed again and explained that the point was protecting a researcher's inventions.

"Oh yah. And what invention are you protecting these days?"

"I'm working on Di-opiomorphine. An application for a patent for a new analgesic, that is."

"And what's your application going to do? Help those guys make a fortune?"

She tried to introduce some nuance. By this point she must already have gotten a good whiff of liquor breath. Georges said, "A real researcher doesn't give a damn about the bucks, my girl, he doesn't need his work to be protected!"

Catherine tried to put in the term "public interest" but to absolutely no avail.

"You folks are the worker bees of the industrial world," Georges went on. "The guys who discovered the AIDS virus didn't give a damn for the money, what interested them was basic research, basic research doesn't need you my darlings, your patent fuss is just commerce plain and simple, you're not protecting anybody, you're protecting the bucks."

He'd cornered her between the window frame and the chest, he was talking into her face from two inches away. She was suffocating and started shouting, "Don't be so aggressive!" People turned around and Pierre stepped in to control his friend. The Manoscrivis took Catherine in hand, making her a plate of salad and bread with the Lallemants' chicken loaf. She kept saying, "Who *is* that guy? He's crazy!" As I passed by Lydie I said, "There's a fellow you ought to do your readjustment thing on!" "Can't adjust an alky," she informed me. I wondered who she did adjust if you couldn't do it to lunatics.

At one point Lambert was heard to say, "All the left-wing ideas are deserting me little by little." To which Jeanne replied, with a boldness that would have been suicidal a few years back among this same bunch, "Me they never did get to!" "Me neither," Lydie chuckled, utterly comfortable among the company. "Lambert neither!" Pierre said. "What are you talking about, my whole life I voted left, through hell and high water!" said Lambert defensively. "People even accuse me of being a hard-core old lefty." Serge claimed the title for himself alone in the room, and someone asked if "lefty" could be translated into other languages. Everyone threw out words, by common consent ruling out the possibility of any real English-language equivalent. Gil Teyo-Diaz, our expert in things Hispanic, offered *"progré,"* citing as he did so the bearded hero of the strip *Quico, el progré.* I said, "And what about in Italian, Jean-Lino—how would you say it?" I saw him redden, embarrassed at being thrust forward suddenly; he looked for a little help from his wife, who shrugged impatiently, he stammered something or other and wound up offering *"sinistroide."*

Sinistroide! The word brought laughter and someone asked if you could say *un vecchio sinistroide.* He said he didn't see why not, but that since he wasn't an Italian from Italy, he wasn't certain of the term, anyhow he couldn't say anything for sure on the matter, the only Italian he spoke was with his cat, and they never discussed politics. This charmed the crowd and he inadvertently became a pet of the evening.

"Youth is departing!" Serge cried when Emmanuel tried to sneak out. The poor kid had to come back into the living room to make the farewell rounds. I had seen him standing before Lydie for a long while, curiously bent over, and then I realized she had taken his hand and was talking to him without releasing it, as do people who are confident of their personal magnetism and whose age allows them some physical familiarity. Catherine asked Jean-Lino if he had any children. His face brightened, he spoke of a joy that had come to him from heaven and Rémi's name reached his lips. Perhaps people invent their joy. Perhaps nothing is real, neither joy nor sorrow. Jean-Lino called "joy" the surprise, the unexpected thing: the presence of a child in his life. He called "joy" the surprise of tending to another being, of being responsible for someone. That's the way Jean-Lino was made. The infernal Rémi was *joy* fallen from heaven.

~

As Emmanuel left, Etienne and Merle Dienesmann arrived. Merle had just performed (she's a violinist) in the Dvořák Requiem at Sainte-Barberino church. Etienne is Pierre's closest friend. For the past few months, his life has been changing. In his garage he is stockpiling light fixtures that he buys because of his late-stage macular degeneration. He categorically refuses to talk about the condition in company and acts as if nothing is wrong (which is becoming less and less possible lately). Their garage has no electricity, so when he enters that enclosure to deposit or to pick up the item that's supposed to help him see, he sees nothing unless he goes in with a thousand-watt flashlight. Etienne was a math professor like Pierre, now he teaches chess to kids for various organizations. I've never heard him complain of his condition. His eyes are losing their brilliance bit by bit, but something else, I don't know how to define it, has come to his face—endurance, nobility. Merle too acts as though nothing is happening, but I see her imperceptibly bring her glass a bit closer to the bottle when Etienne is pouring, or make some other infinitely small gesture that bowls me over.

⌇

Jeanne spent half the party, cellphone and spectacles in hand, absorbed in some feverish conversation. Serge acted like he noticed nothing. Playful, teasing (adorably heavy-handed), bellhop and headwaiter, talking to everyone, even trying to amuse Claudette El Ouardi, he made things light and easy for me. Even if he has got over being jealous of Jeanne's present life, I couldn't understand such crass behavior from her. I found my sister monstrous. A pathetic woman in her gamine spike-heel sandals, indelicate and vulgar. Passing close by her, I said, Stop, be with us a little. She looked at me as if I was embittered and irritating, and she just moved a few steps away. It nearly ruined the evening for me, but then, seeing her from behind—leaning into her phone, her dyed hair tumbling down over her bison-hump back, engulfed for so many years in the banality of life—I thought she was absolutely right to grab at this coxswain-cocksman guy, and the whip and the dirty talk, right to not worry about the jovial ex-husband, about proper behavior, while there was still time.

⌐

Gil Teyo-Diaz and Mimi Benetrof were just back from southern Africa (everyone travels but us). Gil told about how he had found himself nose to nose with not one, not two, but three reclining lions. Man and beasts sized each other up, he said, and none of them budged! "No one budged because the lions were five kilometers away and you were observing them through binoculars from the jeep," Mimi said. We laughed. Danielle laughed, her body stuck to Mathieu Crosse. Then in the far south of Angola, Gil went on, we were in a boat on the Kunene River where it was infested with crocodiles. According to Mimi, they had seen one baby croc on a rock—it might also have been a branch—and it was in northern Namibia. Gil declared that he had taken photos of terrifying crocodiles from less than six feet away. Sure, Mimi said, he took them at the Johannesburg zoo. She's talking nonsense, said Gil, and "anyhow we're not about to go on a trip like that again, now that Mimi isn't earning a cent anymore. My wife works in the reinsurance business, in the department handling Acts of God, the term for natural disasters, which in our times, given the climate craziness, means: Goodbye bonus!" Everyone laughed. The Manoscrivis laughed. That's the picture of them that we've still got: Jean-Lino, in his violet shirt and his new yellow half-round glasses, standing behind the couch, flushed from the champagne or the excitement of being out in society, all his teeth showing. Lydie, seated below him, skirt spread to either side, her face tilted left and laughing hard. Laughing probably the last laugh of her life. A laugh that I ponder endlessly. A laugh without malice, without coquetry, that I still hear resonating with its playful notes—a laugh unthreatened, suspecting nothing, knowing nothing. We get no advance warning of the irremediable. No furtive shadow slipping about with his scythe. When I was little, I used to be fascinated by the hooded skeleton whose dark contours I could see in a lunar halo. I still harbor that idea of premonition, in some form or another—a chill, a light suddenly dimming, a chime—who knows? Lydie Gumbiner did not sense anything coming, any more than the rest of us. When the other guests learned what happened hardly three hours later that night, they were stunned, and frightened. Nor did Jean-Lino feel the faintest grim brush when a few minutes later he started talking mindlessly—infected without realizing it by that conjugal behavior that involves taking center stage and teasing the partner to entertain the group. How could he have sensed anything? The situation felt familiar and inconsequential. Just some Saturday-night silliness—men reshaping the world, kidding around—turning edgy.

Lydie asked whether the chicken in the Lallemants' loaf came from an organic farm source. Sounding a little put out, Marie-Jo replied, "I honestly have no idea. We got it at Truffon."

"Don't know the place," Lydie said.

"It's luscious," said Catherine Mussin.

"Delicious," Danielle confirmed as she sliced a piece, with seductive care, for Mathieu Crosse.

"Have you tried it, Lydie?" I asked.

"No, I don't eat chicken unless I'm sure of its source."

"Well, that's certainly true!" cried Jean-Lino. The Jean-Lino from the racetrack.

"Yes of course it's true," Lydie said tightly. "Besides which, I've just about quit eating meat altogether."

"But she keeps an eye on what other people eat!" Jean-Lino chortled.

"She's right," said Claudette El Ouardi, in one of her few utterances of the evening.

"I'll tell you a story," began Jean-Lino—the racetrack Jean-Lino. "The other night we went out for dinner at the Blue Cartreaux with our grandson Rémi. I was thinking I'd order Basque chicken, and Rémi wanted chicken with fries. Lydie asked the waiter first off if the chickens had been raised on organic feed."

Lydie nodded to confirm the tale.

"When she was told that they were raised on organic feed," Jean-Lino went on, pleased at managing the language, "she asked if the chicken was free-range at the farm, if it had been fluttering around and roosting in the trees. The waiter turns to me, he repeats *Fluttering? In the trees?* with the look of a person dealing with some crank. I gave a little shrug of sympathy, the kind of automatic move us men make sometimes," he joked, "and Lydie repeated, very seriously, that yes, hens do roost."

"Yes, a chicken roosts," Lydie affirmed.

"There, see?" Jean Lino laughed, calling us to witness. "When the waiter left I told Rémi, 'If we want Grandma Lydie to let us order chicken, the chicken has to roost in the trees!' The little guy asked why the chicken had to roost? She says, because it's important for the chicken to have a normal chicken life."

"Exactly," said Lydie.

"We said, 'Yes, yes, that we know, but we didn't know that meant the chicken had to roost in trees!'"

"And it's got to take dust baths, too," Lydie added now, with a stiffened neck and tone of voice that should have chilled Jean-Lino if he'd been more sober.

"Ha ha ha!"

"To groom its feathers. Personally I don't think it's enough to announce, like your friend that stupid waiter who doesn't even know what he's serving, that the chicken ate bio grains, I want to know if the bird has lived a free-range life, in the open air and suited to her species."

"She's right," Claudine El Ouardi said again.

"And I wasn't too pleased, you know, to see you ganging up with the waiter and the boy."

"Oh please, a person's got a right to laugh, the whole business isn't that serious, honeybun! Rémi and I have a new game we play now. Whenever we see the word 'chicken' or hear it, we start fluttering!" he said again, and with his eyes half-shut and his elbows crooked, he flapped his hands at shoulder level, so weirdly that Georges Verbot guffawed—a hoarse, drunken laugh that made everyone uneasy except Jean-Lino, who, in his excitement, improved on his act by stretching out his neck, even emitting (believe it!) a few deep clucks, and rotating his shoulders and back. It was like a kind of incarnation. Georges declared that he was going to work up a new cartoon character—an organic chicken, a next-generation terrorist who'd spread germ warfare—maybe call it "The Devil's Doing"? He could see it already—he would sling a merino wool scarf around its neck . . . Then, leaning into Catherine Mussin who stared back in a panic, he murmured, "You know, merinos? The sheep they shear to hell and mutilate in Australia?"

Thinking about it again now, it seems to me Lydie never opened her mouth for the rest of the evening. Pierre, though he's less given to observing people, has the same impression. At the time, of course, no one paid any attention. It was actually a good party, that Spring Celebration of mine. I said so to myself as I looked around at our friends in the little living room, lounging casually, all of them talking fairly loud, smoking, guzzling food, mixing together. Danielle and Mathieu Crosse cooing out in the hallway, Jeanne and Mimi half-gone, sprawled like teenagers on the hassock giggling quietly. The expression *creating a bond* came to mind again, and I broached the theme of hollow concepts. We came up with a bunch of them, including, oddly, the idea of *tolerance*. It was Nasser El Ouardi who suggested it, declaring that it was a stupid concept to begin with, as tolerance can only be exercised on condition of indifference; once it's no longer tied to indifference, he said, the concept falls apart. Lambert and a few others undertook to defend the term but Nasser, sitting tall above us on the Moroccan chair, held to his viewpoint by taking the notion back to the simple verb "love," arguing with a panache that stumped us. Around eleven o'clock, Pierre's brother Bernard arrived with a Black Forest sausage that could not be sliced. Anyhow, we had long since started on the desserts. He is an engineer for a German company involved in developing an elevator that works without cables and horizontally. My brother-in-law is a great seducer, a love-'em-and-leave-'em guy every woman ought to flee instantly. Catherine Mussin, who has no alert system, instantly signed up for the magnetic levitation. The first guests to arrive were also the first to leave. Hardly had the El Ouardis stood up than Lydie tugged Jean-Lino by the sleeve. I realize now that Jean-Lino was reluctant to go. The El Ouardis and the Manoscrivis parted with an embrace on the doormat where they'd met. There was even some talk of going together, one day soon, to hear Lydie at a *jam session*.

At the end the only people left were the Dienesmanns, Bernard, and us. Bernard started ranting about Catherine Mussin, bawling us out for not coming to his rescue. She apparently told him that she was "in her third season." A woman tells you I'm in my third season, that's a sure cock-strangler, he said. We described her scene with Georges, who got Bernard's full sympathy. And then we talked about the snow again. And about cycles, about the absurdity of believing in linear time, about the past that no longer exists, the present that doesn't exist either. Etienne talked about how, long ago, he used to hike with his father in the mountains; when Merle came along, he and she would pull far ahead of the older man, cutting cross-country, tearing up the slopes—they were *the young folks*. Then later, with their own children, for a long time the two of them still used to walk on ahead of the others. Etienne said, "We'd look back and say, What a drag waiting for you guys to catch up! Today, after a few steps all of us together, the kids are already way out of sight. Uncatchable without even realizing it, the way we must have been. We'd wait for my father at the foot of the hills. When he appeared at the bend of the trail, he would act as if he'd been dawdling on purpose, taking in the beauty. He'd say, Did you see that big field of gentians? And those forget-me-nots? . . . Now it's us who hold up the group," Etienne said. "The details of nature slow us down too. The whole damn thing goes so fast. Anyway, I'll soon have a good excuse with my eyes! . . ." We were content there, the five of us in the nighttime, feet up on the coffee table, at peace and a little old, in the messy apartment. We were content in our world of nostalgias and slow banter, sipping at our pear brandy. I thought how Etienne had been lucky, walking in the mountains with his father. My father wasn't really the sort of guy you could go walking in the mountains with. Or walk anywhere else with, either. And forget about forget-me-nots!

⟋

As he left, Bernard asked who were the woman with the red hair and the guy with the Giscard hairdo? Our upstairs neighbors, we said. They're funny, Bernard said, I like him. We walked out on the balcony to watch the three of them leave the building, Bernard with his motorcycle and his big helmet, the Dienesmanns rounding the corner holding each other by the waist. No trace of snow left, the sky was starry and the air almost gentle.

⟋

I said to Pierre, "Did you think I looked pretty?"
"Very."
"You didn't think Jeanne looked glorious?"
"She looked good."
"Better than me?"
"No, you both looked very good."
"Does she look younger?"
"No, not at all."
"Don't I look younger, though?"
"You look the same."

"If you didn't know me, and you were seeing the two of us, which one would you think was better-looking?"

"What do you say we clean up tomorrow?"

"You'd go spontaneously toward which one of us?"

"You."

"Serge must have told her the same thing in the elevator."

"Mathematics."

"You have no credibility. Did you like her shoes? Aren't those thongs hideous? You don't think it's crazy to dress like that at her age?"

"There's one quiche left . . . Three-quarters of that disgusting chicken loaf."

"It really was disgusting."

"Inedible. I'm tossing it . . . huge rice salad . . . Cheese enough for ten years . . . Nobody touched the liver pâté . . ."

"I forgot to put it out!"

"The Black Forest sausage—you could kill a person with it . . ."

"Toss it. Nice of Lambert to bring you—"

"My edition was earlier."

"Still, nice."

"Yes."

"Georges was already smashed when he came in."

"He's smashed at eight in the morning."

"Why do you invite him?"

"He's all alone."

"He creates a terrible atmosphere."

"Let's go to bed."

We kept up the debriefing in the bathroom.

"Danielle and Mathieu Crosse, you think that could work?" I began again.

"He seems pretty interested, her I don't know."

"I would've said the opposite. I'll call her tomorrow morning."

"Your pal from upstairs, though, la belle Lydie, she's way out there in intergalactic space."

"Oh, you think so!" I laughed. "On a desert island: Claudette El Ouardi or Lydie Gumbiner?"

"Lydie! A hundred times Lydie!"

"Claudette El Ouardi or Catherine Mussin?"

"Claudette. At least you could have a conversation."

"Catherine Mussin or Marie-Jo?"

"That's tough . . . Mussin, with a gag on her mouth. Now you: Georges Verbot or Lambert?"

"No. Impossible."

"You have to."

"Well then—if I wash him and scale his teeth: Georges Verbot."

"Slut."

Once we got to bed, I asked Pierre why we'd never used a whip, or handcuffs and all that. He had a terrible reaction: he laughed. It's true it would make no sense between us. He said, "Georges or Bernard?" I said, Bernard in a blink. He said, "You like him, that jerk!" And that was enough to turn us on.

I was nearly asleep when I heard a noise that sounded like a doorbell. Pierre had put on his miner's headlamp to read an old SAS spy novel (since Gérard de Villiers died, it hurts him not to have new ones to read). I felt him stiffen, but then there was silence. A few minutes later we heard the same sound again. Pierre sat up to listen more closely, he tapped me and whispered, "Somebody's at the door." It was five after two. We both waited, leaning slightly forward, he with his reading lamp still on. Someone was ringing. Pierre got out of bed, he pulled on a T-shirt and undershorts and went to see. Through the peephole he recognized Jean-Lino. He right away imagined a water-pipe break or that sort of thing. He opened the door. Jean-Lino stared at Pierre, he made a strange move with his mouth and then, keeping his lower lip scooped like a bucket, he said, "I killed Lydie." Pierre didn't immediately take in the sentence. He stepped aside to let Jean-Lino in. Jean-Lino entered and stopped still by the door, his arms hanging loose. Pierre too. They both stood waiting in the vestibule. I came in wearing pajamas—a Hello Kitty nightshirt and bottoms in checkered flannel. I said, "What's up, Jean-Lino?" He said nothing, he stared at Pierre. "What's going on, Pierre?" "I don't know. Let's go in the living room." Pierre turned on a lamp and said, "Sit down, Jean-Lino." He offered him the couch where he'd already spent a large part of the evening, but Jean-Lino chose the uncomfortable Moroccan chair. Pierre sat down on the couch and motioned me to come beside him. I was ashamed of the room. We'd been too lazy to clean up. We'd said we'd do it all in the morning. We'd emptied the ashtrays but the place still smelled of cigarettes. There were rumpled napkins, scattered plates, bowls of chips . . . On the chest there was still a row of untouched glasses. I wanted to straighten up a little but I sensed that I ought to sit down. Jean-Lino was higher than us on the Moroccan chair. His comb-over hair hung halfway down on the right side, the other part flapped to the back, it was the first time I'd seen his scalp naked. There was a kind of silence and then I said gently, "What's going on, Jean-Lino?" We watched his mouth. A mouth trying out different shapes. "Bring us a little cognac, Elisabeth," Pierre said.

"For you too?"

"Yes."

I got three vodka glasses and filled them with cognac. Jean-Lino drank his down in one gulp. Something else was strange about his face. Pierre poured him another and we sipped too. I did not understand what the three of us were doing in the middle of the night drinking again in the messy dim living room. After a moment Pierre said, in an ordinary voice as if he were asking a friendly question, "You killed Lydie?" I looked at him, I looked at Jean-Lino, and with a laugh I said, "You killed Lydie!" Jean-Lino set his forearms on the chair frame, but that chair is not made for that, and for a second he looked strapped into an electric chair. I realized he wasn't wearing glasses. I'd never seen him without glasses. "Where is Lydie?" I said.

"I strangled her."

"You strangled Lydie?"

He nodded.

"I don't know what that means."

"What don't you understand? He strangled Lydie," said Pierre.

"Where is she?"

Jean-Lino waved a hand toward the upstairs.

"Is she dead?" Pierre asked.

He nodded and closed his eyes.

"Maybe not," said Pierre. "Let's go check."

Pierre and I stood. I ran into the bedroom to get a sweater and put on slippers. When I got back to the living room Jean-Lino hadn't moved an inch. "Let's go see, Jean-Lino," Pierre encouraged him, "in case she's alive. You know, it's not that easy to strangle someone."

"She's dead," Jean-Lino said in a cavernous voice.

"Not sure, not sure, let's go up!" Pierre was starting to get annoyed. He signaled me to step in. I took Jean-Lino's arm. It was unbelievably stiff and stayed clamped to the Moroccan chair. I tried to reassure him, murmuring kind words. I said, "Jean-Lino, you can't stay in that chair all night."

"Especially since you're the only one who'd ever even want to," Pierre said, trying to tone down the drama.

"That's certainly true," I confirmed.

"Every second counts! We're wasting time!"

"He's right . . ."

"Get hold of yourself, Jean-Lino!"

"I'm telling you, she's dead."

Pierre collapsed back onto the couch, his foot caught in the cord of the table lamp, which fell to the floor and plunged us into near darkness. "Shit, I really need all this!"

I turned on the ceiling light, which we never use. "Not the ceiling light, not the ceiling light, for god's sake!" Pierre moaned. I lit a floor lamp. Jean-Lino faced these successive lighting arrangements without changing his marmoreal posture. I no longer knew what to do, between a husband slumped in the position of a fellow determined to let everything go to hell and a Jean-Lino fossilized and unrecognizable. We'd all had too much to drink. I started tidying the room. I took away the glasses, the bottles, whatever was lying around. I shook out the cloth from the buffet over the balcony edge. I stacked the chairs Lydie had lent us by the door. I brought in the hand vacuum, my beloved Rowenta, to pick up the crumbs. I started to vacuum the coffee table, the carpet beneath it, Pierre emerged from his slack state and snatched it from my hands. "Perfect moment for that! You find this the right time for housekeeping?" He stood up, holding the Rowenta like a machine gun, and said to Jean-Lino, "OK my friend, now we're going upstairs, come on, up we go!" Jean-Lino shifted a little but he seemed nailed to his Moroccan seat, incapable of pulling himself out of it. Pierre set the vacuum going again and aimed it at Jean-Lino's chest, sucking up a patch of shirt with a startling noise. I cried, "What are you doing?" Jean-Lino was terrified by the suction and leapt up into a defense stance. At that moment I knew we were actually going to go upstairs. Jean-Lino set his hair back in place and smoothed it compulsively several times, I gently led him toward the door. Pierre put on street shoes and we left the apartment. We went up on foot, by the yellowish light of the stairwell, Pierre ahead in pale pink flared undershorts, naked legs and loafers, then Jean-Lino in his rumpled party clothes, and me at the rear in pajamas and fake-fur slippers. At their door, Jean-Lino fumbled in his pockets before pulling out the right key, we could hear Eduardo meowing and scratching behind the door, Jean-Lino murmured little words to him, *sono io gioia mia, sta' tranquillo cucciolino*. I took Pierre's hand, I felt a little anxiety and at the same time a terrific desire to move forward into the thickness of the night.

⌇

We went in. He did not turn on the vestibule light. Eduardo slithered among our legs with his back arched in a dromedary hump. At the end of the corridor, the bathroom and the bedroom were lighted. Jean-Lino took up the same waiting posture again—shoulders hunched high, arms hanging loose—as in our house at the same location.

"Where is she?" Pierre whispered. I found the whispering bizarre and at the same time I understood that there was no way we could talk at normal volume. Jean-Lino tilted his head toward the bedroom. Pierre moved into the hallway. With me behind him. From the hall we could already see her. Feet up by the head of the bed, skirt rumpled, dressed still as she had been at our house. Pierre pushed the door wider. She was lying with her jaw hanging open, her eyes wide and bulging beneath the poster of Nina Simone in her white string dress and her endless pendants. We saw right away that it was very serious. In a surge of professionalism (from TV serials? police thrillers?) Pierre gripped her wrist to check the pulse. Jean-Lino appeared in the doorway, nodding his head like a witness gloomily gratified at seeing his first impression confirmed. He had his sand-colored glasses on again. Pierre looked at Jean-Lino in alarm. He said, "You really did . . . She is dead." Jean-Lino agreed. No one moved. Then Pierre said, "Maybe we should . . . maybe close her eyes."

"Yes . . ."

"I'll let you do it . . ."

Jean-Lino came over to Lydie and swiped his hand over her eyelids, a gesture from a religious drawing. But the jaw still hung open. I said, "Can't we put it a little better . . . ?" Jean-Lino opened a drawer where there were all sorts of scarves. I picked up the first I saw, a sheer veil with a pattern of pale flowers. Jean-Lino pressed the mouth closed, I wrapped the head and tied the knot hard beneath the chin. She was much more pleasant to look at now. She looked as if she were taking a little nap outdoors under a tree. And then, I don't know why, Jean-Lino also put shoes on her feet, red pumps with straps and a flat bow. I looked at those extremities on top of the trapunto bedcover, it was unthinkable that those feet and the ankle bracelet with the dangling charms should no longer belong to a person. I was startled to find myself framing the image in my head: from the hem of the dress to the edge of the bed, showing a few inches of wall, the slim legs, the satin-clad feet splayed on the puckered fabric as if after some brutal lovemaking. The already-past image of Lydie Gumbiner. One of the charms was longer than the others, I didn't have my glasses on but I thought I could make out some kind of owl. What had that bird meant, dangling against her skin? On the dresser there was another owl, in pewter. To bear life on earth we gather magical objects. This is what enchants me when I look at the stop-time world of photographs, those details like elegies. Clothes, knickknacks, talismans, all the bits of chic or shabby paraphernalia provide silent sustenance to mankind. Pierre said, "Now we've got to call the police, Jean-Lino."

"The police—ah no—no no."

Pierre glanced at me. I asked, "But what do you mean to do? . . ."

"No, not the police."

"Jean-Lino, you've . . . This thing did happen to you . . . You came to get us . . . What can we do for you?"

Pierre was standing next to a chest, the gravity of his tone and the prayer-position of his hands a little undercut by his pink skirt-like underwear. Jean-Lino, his head lowered, was watching the cat's movements around the bed.

"You want us to phone someone? A lawyer? I know a lawyer."

Eduardo climbed onto the chamber pot. A porcelain chamber pot with a round wooden lid on top (a cheese platter?) and I thought how that wasn't a bad idea, a chamber-pot at the foot of the bed, what with me getting up three times a night to pee. Jean-Lino said *Non sul vaso da notte micino* with a little caress meant to make the cat get down. Eduardo ignored him, busy as he was with scrutinizing Lydie's body from precisely the same level as the view, "*Ti ha fatto male, eh, piccolino mio . . .*"

"Jean-Lino, you're going to have to cooperate a little," Pierre began again.

"Let's go into the living room, maybe?" I said.

"*Povero patatino . . .*"

Pierre went to glance out the window. He closed the drapes. In his duckskin loafers and sheer underpants, he declared: "OK, I'll tell you what, Jean-Lino, if you don't call the police, at some point we're going to do it."

"It's not for us to do it!" I protested.

"It's not for us to do. But someone has to do it."

"Let's not stay in this room, let's go think it over calmly."

"Think about what, Elisabeth? That woman's been strangled by her husband, a fit of passion, no one's asking for details, the police have to be called. And you, Jean-Lino, come on back to earth. And say something, in a language a person can understand, because this lovetalk with that fucking Italian cat is beginning to get on my nerves."

"He's in shock."

"He's in shock, yes. We're all in shock."

"Let's try not to get upset, Pierre . . . Jean-Lino, what do you propose? . . . Jean-Lino? . . ."

Pierre sat down in the yellow velvet armchair. Jean-Lino pulled the pack of Chesterfields out of his pocket and lit one. The smoke spread over Lydie. He immediately tried to wave it away with his hand. And then, looking at his wife with what I thought was sorrow, he said, "Could I speak to you alone for two seconds, Elisabeth?"

"What do you want to say to her?"

"Just two seconds, Pierre."

I made a little sign like, the situation is under control, and I took Jean-Lino's arm to draw him out of the bedroom. Jean-Lino plunged into the bathroom and closed the door behind me. In a very muffled voice and without turning on any light, he said:

"Could you help me put her into the elevator? . . ."

"But . . . what do you mean?"

"In a suitcase . . ."

"In a suitcase? . . ."

"She's tiny, she doesn't weigh much . . . Someone has to go down with her . . . I can't go in the elevator."

"Why go with her?"

"To handle the arrival downstairs. In case someone had rung for it from there." That made sense to me.

"You'll do what with her? . . ."

"I know where to take her . . ."

"You're going to drive her somewhere in the car?"

"The car's right out front. Just help me get her down, Elisabeth, I'll take care of the rest . . ."

There was a familiar smell of laundry soap. We were standing in utter darkness. I couldn't see him. I could hear the urgency and distress in his voice. I thought how we'd have to be sure the parking lot was empty too . . . The door was wrenched open.

"You're thinking of helping this nut to stick his wife in the elevator, Elisabeth?" Pierre gripped my arm with steel fingers (he has beautiful hands, and strong). "We're going downstairs and I'm calling the police."

He was pulling me, I resisted by clutching some bathrobes hanging from a hook—this lasted maybe three seconds. We must have set off some switch because a neon wall fixture went on. Everything turned yellow, that old-time yellow like we used to have in Puteaux.

"Go, Elisabeth, go on back to your place my dear Elisabeth, I'm crazy, you should leave here," Jean-Lino implored with his arms stretched before him.

"But what will you do, Jean-Lino?" I said.

He put his head in his arms and sat down on the edge of the bathtub. Rocking slightly and without looking at us, he groaned, "I'll get hold of myself, I'll get hold of myself." I felt insanely sad for him, huddled like that, his hair a mess, beneath a laundry wall rack in the crowded bathroom.

Pierre started to pull at me again. I said, "Stop pulling me!"

"You want to go to jail? You want to get us all thrown in jail?"

Without looking at us, and with great effort like a child being scolded, Jean-Lino said, "She kicked Eduardo."

"Lydie kicked Eduardo?!?" I repeated.

"She kicked the cat and he strangled her. And we're out of here," Pierre said.

"But she adores animals!" I said.

Jean-Lino shrugged.

"She had me sign a petition this very afternoon!"

"What petition did you sign?" Pierre demanded to know.

"A petition against grinding up baby chicks."

"OK, OK, that's enough," Pierre said, furious and pushing me toward the hall door.

Fur bristling and teeth bared, Eduardo slipped out of the bathroom.

"*Non aver paura, tesoro* . . . He's got kidney stones, the poor thing."

"Are you going to call the police, Jean-Lino?" I asked. "It's got to be you who does it."

"There's no other solution," Pierre said.

"Yes . . ."

"None, Jean-Lino."

"Yes."

Pierre opened the front door and shoved me out onto the landing. Before he closed it, I called in, "Do you want someone to stay with you?"

"Wake up the whole building!" Pierre whispered, carefully closing the door. Then he pulled me into the stairwell, gripping me with his steel hand. Back in our apartment he kept me moving on into the living room as if to avoid our being heard. He tried to draw the drapes, which are purely decorative, and tore off a corner of one.

"What the hell are you doing, Pierre?"

"Those stupid panels!" He tossed down a glassful of cognac. "You were ready to help him get rid of the body, Elisabeth?"

"It's offensive, you coming to eavesdrop at the door."

"You were ready to take the elevator with a corpse . . . Can you see yourself going down alone, four floors with a stiff? . . . Answer me please."

"In a suitcase."

"Oh, all right then—excuse me!"

"You would have known that if you'd been a little patient."

"You realize what we're discussing? This is really serious, Elisabeth."

I was suddenly cold, and my head hurt. I put on a shawl and went to heat some water in the kitchen. I came back with my tea and huddled in a corner of the couch, at the opposite end from where the Manoscrivis had sat. Pierre strode around the room. I said, "I think it's awful we've abandoned him." He sat beside me and rubbed my shoulder, a gesture that could have been intended either to warm me up or to calm a crazed mind.

On the other side of the parking lot the building was entirely dark. We must have been the only people who had not surrendered to the night. We and the upstairs neighbors.

Lydie, watched over by the black cat, stretched out in her party dress, and Jean-Lino abandoned beneath the hanging laundry. In a storybook I used to have, the princess pricked herself with a spindle and fell into a deep sleep. They had her laid out on a bed embroidered with gold and silver, she had those same coral-colored tresses and her lips were like a red red rose. A text came up on my phone.

Pierre said, "You're not answering him!"

"But it's your son!"

Emmanuel had written "Great spring celebration, Mom!" with a smiley face and a snowman. That sent me into tears, without understanding why. That message in the middle of the night. The snowman. The little figure of happiness that sends you right back to everything that ends, to loss. The children are way out ahead, like the children of Etienne and Merle on the mountain trail. As I had hurled myself far away, so far, from my parents. It's not the big betrayals but the repeated tiny losses that make for the melancholy. When Emmanuel was small, he ran a shop. A little low table, in a corner of his bedroom, where the merchandise was laid out and where he sat behind it. He would sell things he made himself, all kinds of cardboard items painted in decorative patterns, rollers from Sapolin paint and toilet paper, finds picked up outdoors, acorns and twigs he also painted, little figures in modeling clay. He had made his own currency—the "pestos"—just bills, bits of paper torn any whichway. Every day he would call out from his room, "The store is open!" Neither Pierre nor I would react; we'd got used to the call. He never repeated it, so a long silence would follow. Then there'd come a moment when I remembered that I'd heard him, and I'd picture him all alone there, the little businessman behind his counter, waiting for the customer. I'd go in, carrying the purse with pestos bills in it. He was pleased to see me arrive but quite professional nonetheless—we said the formal *vous* to each other. I would make my selection, pay for it, and leave with my bag of river pebbles and painted chestnuts, faces on the white discs smiling or scowling. On that list of hollow concepts we had put *the duty to remember*. What an inept expression! Time past, good or bad, is nothing but an armful of dead leaves we should just burn up. We'd also listed *the work of mourning*. Two expressions utterly empty of meaning, and contradictory besides. I asked Pierre, "What shall I say?"

"You can tell him the neighbor bumped off his wife an hour later."

"Anyhow, he thinks we're asleep."

We pulled the shawl over us both as if we were expecting to spend the night on the sofa. Suddenly he got up, I heard him bustling in the entryway. He came back with the toolbox and the stepladder, which he unfolded at the window. I watched him climb the rungs in his panty-skirt and his loafers. Driven by some feverish energy, he tried to repair the curtain rod. The rollers were caught in the rod and the fabric hem was torn. He tried to patch it together. Scrabbling in the toolbox, he asked me whether we had any extra hooks. I said I had no idea. He got irritated, tugged at the cord, pulled on the linen panel and sprang all the hooks, and wound up tearing the whole thing down in a fury. I had no reaction. Pierre sat on the top of the stepladder, hunched over, belly hanging forward, hands crossed, elbows on his thighs. We stayed like that for a strange moment, without speaking. I was suddenly overcome by a crazy giggle, a thing at the back of the throat that I more or less stifled in a cushion. He stepped down, folded the ladder, and put it back in the entry closet with the toolkit. Coming back to the living room he said, "I'm going to bed."

"Yes."

"Let's go to bed."

"Yes . . ."

Jean-Lino's little bouquet of mauve roses was jammed into a glass of water on the edge of a bookshelf. I hadn't even bothered to take off their string. I looked for another vase and in the end I put them into a perfume flask. When he and I visited the aunt in her rest home, Jean-Lino had bought a bouquet of anemones. He told me, "You give them to her." I held the bouquet as I stood in a corridor waiting for the aunt. There were wooden railings along either side, a woman was walking backward with a cane and thick pressure stockings. The aunt had appeared with her walker and charged right toward the cafeteria. I presented the flowers awkwardly, the aunt had no interest in cut flowers from Paris; they stayed behind in the commons room. Now I set the perfume flask on the coffee table. The roses seemed fake. The whole arrangement in that stained crystal vase had the look of an ornament on a gravestone. Or maybe it was just a sense of anomaly because of the hour and the situation. What was Jean-Lino doing all alone up there? Pierre called to me from the bedroom. I said, "I'm coming"... How could we have left him there?

He had taken Pierre and me to the Courette du Temple, one of those cafés that become jazz clubs three times a week. He had organized everything—that is, arriving a half hour ahead of the show, in a room nearly empty except for the musicians at the bar. Wall speakers played standards over an array of small round tables. Jean-Lino, dressed all "casual," had seated us practically on the edge of a tiny stage holding a piano, a bass, and drums. We said "So close?" But he wanted us to see Lydie without the obstruction of a pillar or other spectators. I think, rather, that he needed to assert *his* place each time, his inaugural location. He immediately greeted the owner, made the introductions as an insider, ordered three drinks without asking our choice. People gradually arrived, people of all ages, in unfashionable outfits. I remember one fellow with silver-dyed hair tied into a tall do, coming and going in a jacket with a sheepskin collar over a red shirt. Some people wrote their names on a slate that hung from a mike stand; they were signing up (to perform) for the

jam session, Jean-Lino explained. Lydie arrived glowing
and effervescent, rushing to sign the schedule slate even
before she came to join us. At first the musicians played
on their own, then the trumpeter sang "I Fall in Love
Too Easily." I mused that it had been a long time since I
fell in love *easily*, and it was also a long time since I had
sat with a bunch of strangers in that seedy heat. After
that, the singers came onstage carrying their sheet music.
We clapped nicely no matter the performance. Jean-
Lino was the biggest applauder. A woman in a polka-dot
dress completely wrecked "Mack the Knife" in German;
the man with the sheepskin collar (my favorite, I still
think about him), introduced by the trumpeter as "Greg,"
launched into a song he'd written himself. Gestures of
rejection, caressing the mike, nods of quiet approval for
the trumpet's occasional contributions—he was meeting
the world head-on and alone, the shiny silver helmet just
a foot or two from us. Jean-Lino clapped hard, Lydie
quivered with empathy. She knew him, a regular, in
real life he was a ticket collector on the SNCF. She was
applying fresh lip gloss when the trumpeter announced,
"And now, we'll hear... Lydie!!" Jean-Lino turned
toward Pierre, with whom he'd never made any particular connection, and gripped his shoulder. He was red,
maybe from the liquor, or stage fright, or a swell of pride
that also had him scanning the audience to assess the
level of concentration. Lydie began *Les Moulins de mon
coeur* in an intimate tone, her voice nearly a murmur,

before filling her lungs for the *"anneau de Saturne"* and the *"ballon de carnaval."* In the full-front spotlight, the wild cap of curls and the sparkling earloops glittered. She had a delicate voice whose timbre sounded young to me, its inflections slightly naïve against her physical figure and the sense of harsh energy she gave off. She sang *"Les Moulins de mon coeur"* without drawing out the words, like a simple country song heard along the road, not meant to go anywhere, just to pass the time. This was an odd girl, someone you might have run across in a very different place and time. You had to see Jean-Lino. In the grip of joy, nearly risen off his chair. She didn't look at him. Maybe didn't care about him. She sang the words of abandonment with a child's lightness—the bird tumbling from the nest, footprints fading—as she rocked from foot to foot, setting her bracelet's charms swaying, living the moment to its depth with a regal imperturbability. Jean-Lino, leaning forward, watched over his idol with his body straining, expecting nothing in return. At one point he sensed me observing him and he straightened up as if caught in some misstep, smiling happy and embarrassed. To save face he snapped a photo of Lydie from the telephone set on the table, a quick one, not bothering with framing, his enchantment so pure he never supposed any need for it. We clapped noisily, the three of us. I knew Pierre was bored but he joined in politely. It seemed to me that the other customers appreciated Lydie too. She stayed at the mike awhile, lingering, taking her time before giving over her place, unlike the other performers, who had fled timidly the minute they were done. Before he went out for a smoke, Jean-Lino ordered four glasses of Saint James rum. Pierre had sent me a few desperate signals that made me giggle. Lydie came back to her seat in full bloom, fanning her low neckline. The trumpeter was saying, "And now we'll hear . . . Jean-Jacques!!" It was a good-hearted evening fated for forgetting, just one in the flow of life's numberless evenings.

That place, the Courette du Temple, seems distant now— the woman in the polka-dot dress, the man who thought he could play "Fly Me to the Moon" on the harmonica. The four of us, drunk on the sidewalk, crowding into and then thrown out of a cab that was already occupied. A man who'd been among the first to perform asked me, "You come here often?"

"First time."

"The first time, people don't dare."

The past falls apart so quickly! It turns to chalk and crumbles like the Wall of the

Forgotten. I often think of the San Michele cemetery in Venice. We visited there, Pierre and Bernard and I, nearly alone one foggy November day. San Michele, an endless maze of enclosures, cells, plots, fields. An entire island of tombs. The walkways in the columbarium: whole walls of photo portraits bristling with jutting flasks of artificial flowers. Hundreds of photos of people dressed in their best, tidily coiffed, smiling gaily. We'd got lost there, wandering vaguely about seeing nobody else. It was lunchtime, midweek. On one tombstone there was this inscription: *You will be with us always, Love, your Emma.* I was struck by the nerve of the phrase. As if certain people remained eternally on earth. As if the two worlds should go on separately. In the urns section there was that Wall of the Forgotten. A dingy gray surface. The names and dates on it were nearly obliterated. You could still read "1905" on one of the clearer plaques. No photo, nowhere—there was nothing, just one or two clumps of porcelain flowers jutting from a crack in the slab. These people were no longer *with* anyone in our world. The black-and-whitish coloring of that wall—I see it as the very color of the past. From the minute you set foot on earth you must give up any idea of permanence. Near the Rialto bridge, on that same foggy day, Pierre bought me a short cashmere cape, brown and blue. I'd spotted it on a dummy in the window of a poorly lit shop. The door was hard to open and the man who came to help us had a half-paralyzed arm. An enormous counter ate up the whole interior. On the walls, shelving held merchandise, almost all of it wrapped in bundles. With his good arm he drew from a drawer several capes of different colors in their transparent slipcases. None was the same nice match of colors. When he understood that he would have to get down the one from the shopwindow, he grumbled something toward the rear of the shop. A woman arrived, no more cheerful than he, her head sunk between her shoulders, dressed as if she were outdoors (it was chilly in the shop). She moved a stool to reach into the vitrine and set about undoing the pins that attached the cape to the figure. I tried on the cape at a mirror where you couldn't see a thing. I turned toward the men. Pierre thought it wasn't bad. Bernard thought it looked a bit matronly. The couple said absolutely nothing. They seemed old and uninterested. We bought the cape, very inexpensive. The woman folded it carefully and put it in a pretty slipcase, which I still have, with *Cashmere Made in Italy* printed on it. They evinced no pleasure from the sale, which might have been the only one all day. They must have been there for years, seen their clientele thin out little by little, the elegant inhabitants of the neighborhood leaving town or dead. When they themselves go, Chinese shopkeepers will take over the place and sell handbags. The same colored leather bags hanging on display everywhere in the city. Or else an ice cream parlor, with super-harsh neon lighting. Or else, although not very likely, some young folks will open a dress shop. But the dress shop is part of the same transitory world as the handbags. The disagreeable couple belonged to a slower human race. I say slower, not more enduring.

They were someplace in the landscape, they still go on existing a little in my memory.

At Pasteur, our department is in a building that was once the hospital. It was built early in the twentieth century and it's landmarked. It's made of stone and red brick, in the style of the historic building. The two wings are separated by gardens and linked by a marvelous green-house, no longer in use because the glass structure could collapse. Still, the plants go right on growing there like in a little jungle. The window of my own ground-floor office looks onto a hedge and trees. Beyond them is a newer building with a glass façade. On days when the sun shines the façade of our own is reflected in it. I day-dream, I travel back, imagining the life there in the old days when contagious patients were kept in isolation, there were wooden beds and nurses in stiff caps or white veils. I see things I did not see before.

After a while I no longer heard a sound from our bed-room. I went to look. Pierre was burrowed in on his side. He'd fallen asleep. Asleep. While just above, on the other side of the ceiling ... I sat on the edge of the bed and looked at his graying hair. I really like his hair. It's thick and wavy. I stroked it. He was sleeping. That disturbed me. He himself said, later, that he was knocked out by the series of shots we'd drunk in our panic and disarray all evening long. No matter. He'd gone to bed, he'd pulled up the covers, he'd settled into the position of a man consenting to sleep. He had left me all alone. Unsupervised. He had come to take me back with his steel fingers for nothing. I was willing to obey the paternal voice as long as it stayed firm. The stern voice had scolded for a couple of brief minutes and then let the matter go. A sleeping guy is a guy who's dropped you. He's no longer worrying about you. I had thought him a little ridiculous as the stern taskmaster ready to phone the cops, but I did think, Well, he's afraid for me, he's protecting me. Actually, he had herded me back into the fold and then washed his hands of me. No worry, no concern for another person. One more unkept promise. And what should I make of—I thought, there on the edge of the bed in the dark—what should I make of his lack of curiosity? Pierre had never been interested in crime stories in the news, in the troubles of common folk. He sees no shadowy dimension there. For him it all smells of piss or these people are garbage. In a way I'm closer to Ginette Anicé than I am to my husband. I went into the bathroom. I sat on the toilet seat and examined the samples I'd been given along with the Gwyneth Paltrow anti-aging product. There was a nutrient mask from the Dead Sea that you leave on to work through the night. I put it on, thoughtfully. No clear ideas. The other day on TV I heard some not-old fellow say, "The Lord guides me, each day I ask

his advice, even before coming here on the program."
God does a lot of advising these days. I remember a time
when such a remark would have provoked wild laughter.
Today everyone considers it normal, including on the
intellectual TV talk shows. I would like someone to help
me out, or enlighten me. Here in the bathroom I had
nobody, not even a double like Danielle's who would
call me "hey girl." I went to the front door and looked
through the peephole. Total darkness. I went back into
the living room, I turned off the lamp and opened the
window. I stood at an angle to the balcony. No one in the
parking lot. The Manoscrivis' Laguna, parked just below.
I listened to the silence of the damp night, a touch of
wind, a car engine. I closed the window again. No sound
came from upstairs. Nothing. I started prowling the
living room, tracing pointless rounds in my fake-fur slippers. I caught myself doing a few little skips among the
furniture. Despite it all, something in me was dancing. I
had known that effect before, that irrepressible lightness
at a moment when the full force of misfortune has just
missed you. Is it a kind of drunkenness at reprieve? At
the sense of keeping your footing on a pitching deck?
or just stupidly, as for Ginette Anicé (her again), at
escaping boredom? In the program for the night there
was suddenly the chance to go off-piste. My husband
having abandoned me, I could just as easily go back into
the stairwell. It's not a bad thing that an expectation is
disappointed—the space of disappointment is where our

Faustian gene gets expressed. According to Svante Pääbo, one of my biology professors, we diverge from the Neanderthals by only an infinitely small modification in a particular chromosome. An odd mutation in the genome that might enable a thrust into the unknown, the crossing of the oceans with no certainty of finding land beyond the horizon, the whole human fever of exploration, of creativity and of destruction. In other words: a gene for madness. I went back into our bedroom. Pierre was sleeping deeply. I grabbed a cardigan lying there, took the keys from the vestibule, and quietly left the flat. Upstairs, I knocked as I whispered Jean-Lino's name. He opened the door, unsurprised, a syringe in his hand. The place smelled of smoke. I'm in the middle of doing the medications, he said. For a moment I thought he was talking about Lydie and that he'd lost his mind. Following him into the kitchen, I understood that he meant Eduardo. "He has kidney stones. He has to take six pills a day and a new diet of fish patties that's not helping him at all," said Jean-Lino, bustling about. "Please sit down, Elisabeth."

"The poor baby."

"The first day, I spent an hour and a half getting him to swallow one antibiotic tablet. The vet told me You just stick the pill in his mouth and you hold his jaws closed. Oh sure. The minute I let go of his jaw he'd spit it out. I understood that to swallow, a cat has to open and close his jaws, as if he's chewing. But the worst part," Jean-Lino said, "is the yeast."

As he spoke, he was pouring a mixture he had previously spoon-stirred from the bowl into a baby's nursing syringe.

"Those fish patties give him diarrhea. The vet says it's not them, but I say it is. A urinary-stress formula. He gobbles them up in half a second, he adores them, and they give him diarrhea. The antibiotics and the anti-kidney-stone things, I've figured out a system. They're real tiny, about the size of a lentil, but the Ultradiar capsule, I have to dissolve that in water and feed it to him with the baby syringe. OK, where'd he go, the little *diablo*? I'll go look for him."

I stayed on for a moment alone in the kitchen. On the table was a circular with Lydie's picture. LYDIE GUMBINER Musicotherapy, Sonotherapy, Massage with Tibetan bowls. In the foldover section there was the photo of a gong, and below it, the line *The voice and the rhythm matter more than the words and the meaning.* I looked at the straw basket on the countertop with its cotton Provençal neckerchief, I put a name to all the herbs in the collection—garlic, thyme, onion, oregano, sage, bay laurel. Charmingly arranged by a caring hand, I said to myself. With some dish in mind? or just to make theater of daily life? Jean-Lino returned with Eduardo in his arms. He sat down and began to feed him the solution the way you'd give a bottle to a newborn. I'm never comfortable in the presence of that cat, a savage little thug, but now he looked beaten down, accepting the treatment and the humiliating position with fatalism.

"This is the hard part," Jean-Lino said, "you've got to be very careful he doesn't swallow the wrong way." Was it that line? The almost pedagogic posture of his body? I had the sneaking sense that he was preparing Eduardo's immediate future. In short, that he was hoping to entrust the cat to us. That threw me into a panic. I said, "What do you mean to do, Jean-Lino?"

"The day before yesterday, he drank too fast and he started coughing, coughing, choking."

"What do you mean to do about Lydie?"

"I'm going to call the police."

"Yes. Of course."

"Where's Pierre?"

"He went to sleep."

The cat was calmly drinking its yeast. The box of fish patties sat on the table. Given the label, I thought there must be some sort of anti-anxiety drug in the formula. Jean-Lino was still leaning his head against the animal's muzzle. His voice had grown stronger since he appeared at our door. The look of his face and his mouth, too. I had known the champion of The Mouth in Search of a Form: Michel Chemama, my English teacher at the Lycée Auguste Renoir, a Jew from Algeria, forever linked to the words "Haaarvestiiing meuchiiiine," pronounced with the lower lip thrust forward (for years, and still today, I have puzzled over the urgency of teaching the term "harvesting machine" to French city kids just beginning to learn English). Jean-Lino set the syringe down on the table. Eduardo slipped to the floor and left the kitchen. We did not speak. I really liked Michel Chemama, always in his gray flannel trousers, his double-breasted navy blazer with its metal buttons. He may still be alive. As a child you can't judge a teacher's age, they all seem old. It was nice of you to come back, Jean-Lino said. What happened, Jean-Lino? I wouldn't have chosen to be so direct, but nothing else came to mind. Language transmits only the obstacles to expression. You're aware of that in normal circumstances and you work around it. Jean-Lino shook his head. He leaned forward to pick up a mandarin orange from the counter. He offered me one. I refused. He began to peel his. I said, "The two of you looked happy at home."

"No."

"No?"

"Well, yeah—*I* was."

"Don't feel you have to—"

He set the mandarin down on a bit of the peel, pulled apart a segment and took off the threads of white pith.

"I don't feel anything now. Am I a monster, Elisabeth?"

"You're anesthetized."

"I cried when it happened. But I don't know if it was from sadness."

"Not yet."

"Ah—yes . . . Yes, that's it. Not yet."

He took up, one after the other, the orange sections and cleaned them without eating them. I was dying to ask him, What do you plan to do with Eduardo, but I was afraid of immediately easing his way by my question. I also wanted to ask him about his new glasses. A person doesn't change unthinkingly from dark rectangle to sand-colored half-round. The thick frames still hinted at his baby face. Among the unknowable elements that cause you to move toward a person and love him, there's the face. But no facial description is possible. I looked at the long nose that lifted and spread at the tip, the long part underneath, a straight line down from nostrils to mouth. I thought about his teeth, going every which-way, the complete opposite of today's dental style. While he fiddled with the orange peel, I registered forever the three things Jean-Lino's face expressed all at the same time: goodness, suffering, gaiety. I said, "I never saw those glasses before."

"They're new."

"They're nice."

"They're from Roger Tin. Acetate."

We smiled. For sure, it was Lydie who'd chosen the glasses. He would never have reached for that fashion color on his own. There was a racket from the bedroom. I leapt to my feet and pressed my body absurdly against the fridge. Jean-Lino went to see. I was ashamed of my reaction. I mean, if Lydie had actually waked up that would be good news, why be frightened? No, no, the dead awakening has always been terrifying, all of literature says so. I stood in the kitchen doorway and listened. Unalarming sounds, Jean-Lino's Italian voice. I heard him close the door to the bedroom, the corridor plunged into darkness, and he reappeared. Eduardo had tried to jump from the chamber pot to the night table but the lid had slid off, he missed the jump and knocked over the bed lamp. Jean-Lino sat down at the table again. So did I. He took out a Chesterfield. "May I?"

"Of course."

"He's got no experience there—normally he's not allowed in the bedroom."

I did something I hadn't done in thirty years. I took a cigarette and lit up. I drew the smoke right into my lungs. It snagged at my throat and I found the taste disgusting. Sometimes during school vacation, Joelle and I would go to stay near her family's place in the Indre. They would lend us a little farmhouse outside Le Blanc. We'd say, "We're off to see the yokels." One night at supper my right arm started to twitch in a kind of Saint Vitus' dance, I couldn't pick up a fork, I'd smoked two packs of Camels in the course of the day, I was thirteen. Later I smoked again a little with Denner. Jean-Lino took the cigarette out of my hand and stubbed it out in the promotional ashtray. I dared to do another thing I would never have done any other time: I stroked his pitted cheek. I said, "What's that from?"

"My scars?"

"Yes . . ."

"Acne. I used to be covered with pimples."

He smoked gazing around the kitchen. What was he thinking about? Me, I was picturing Lydie stretched out dead in the other room. It was both enormous and nothing at the same time. The house was calm. The Frigidaire was sending out its hum. When we were emptying our mother's apartment, my sister and I found a bunch of her office supplies in a drawer. The stuff was years old, from when she kept the accounts at the Sani-Chauffe company. A case holding a ruler, a four-color Bic pen, staples, a brand-new ream of paper, scissors that could cut for the next hundred years. Objects are bastards, Jeanne said. Again I asked Jean-Lino what had happened.

When they got upstairs, Lydie accused him of humiliating her in company. That he could go back over the episode at the Carreaux Bleus restaurant with his caricature of the chicken was a betrayal in itself, plus the fact of mixing Rémi up in the story. He shouldn't have mentioned Rémi, Lydie said, and certainly not to report that the boy had made fun of her, his grandmother, which besides wasn't true. Jean-Lino, still in euphoric spirits, replied breezily that he hadn't meant any harm, that he'd told that whole story carried away by the hope of making people laugh, which often happens at parties like that, and in fact everybody did laugh good-humoredly. He reminded her how even she had wound up laughing, back there in the restaurant when they'd imitated hens fluttering. Lydie flew into a rage, claiming that she had only laughed (and not much) to cover for him, Jean-Lino, in the boy's eyes—to keep the child from realizing, given his ultrasensitivity, how upsetting the imitation was. She would never have imagined, she added, that on top of that she would have to relive that ridicule among strangers, and she pointed out that the performance at the party was applauded only by that belligerent drunk. She scolded him for not seeing her stiffness or her subtle signals, and generally for a lack of sensitivity toward her. Jean-Lino tried to protest, because if there was ever a man attentive to her, and even on the alert, it was he, but Lydie was immured in her complaints and would have none of it. That chicken story, told—alas yes—with the sole purpose of setting off some stupid laughter, revealed his insensitivity, not to say his mediocrity. She had always accepted that he chose not to adopt her way of life, as long as she felt respected and understood. Which was obviously not the case. Yes, some creatures do have wings instead of arms! And thus they flutter and roost. At least—she added as if aiming at Jean-Lino himself—they do as long as the cowardice and thoughtlessness of men didn't make it impossible for them to do so. What was funny about that? She didn't understand how people could laugh at lives that are miserable from birth to the slaughterhouse. And drag a child of six into the laughter, to make him into the torturer of tomorrow. Animals only want to live, to peck, to munch grass in the fields. Men throw them into terrible confinement, into factories of death where they can't move, or turn around, or see daylight, she said. If he really cared out the boy's welfare and not just winning him over with some loathsome attitudes, these are the things he should be teaching him. Animals have no voice and can't demand anything for themselves, but by luck, she boasted, there were people in the world like Grandma Lydie to register complaints on their behalf: that's what he could have taught Rémi, instead of making fun of her. Generally speaking, she blamed him for coming on to the boy at her expense (Jean-Lino took offense at the term, completely wrong, a term she chose just to mortify him needlessly)—the only strategy he could find, she said, to work up a little complicity with him. She said his behavior was pathetic, that he meant nothing, absolutely nothing, to the boy and would never be his Grampa Lino. She said she was outraged that he should call him *our* grandchild when he was nothing to the child, who did have actual grandfathers even though one was dead and he never saw the other one. That such a usurpation, especially in front of her, and among strangers, was an act of great violence, since he knew perfectly well her position on the matter and he'd used the term so casually in a situation where she couldn't correct him. She said further that he didn't realize it but the child despised him, because children have no respect for people who try to please them and who do anything they want, especially that kind of child, she said, matured beyond his age by the circumstances of life and endowed with a superior intelligence. When Jean-Lino tried to cite the recent signs of affection Rémi had shown him, she was quick to say that all children, Rémi no less than any other, are little whores. And on the pretext of disabusing him, she took the occasion to remind him of his inexperience in that realm. She said that a man who went dotty like that lost all sex appeal for any normal woman and that she had seen quite enough of that behavior already over Eduardo. That she had managed despite herself to put up privately with the spectacle of his regression, but had never expected to see it play out in plain daylight. "In a couple," she said, "each party has got to make some effort to do the other honor. How a person conducts himself affects what people will think of his or her partner. What good are the violet shirt and the Roger Tin frames if he goes off on dwarf arms and clucking? When I put on my coral earrings and my red Gigi Dool shoes, when I cancel two patients to get a hair coloring and a manicure on the very morning of a party, I do it to measure up to what I believe Your Wife should be, I do it to honor you. And that goes for every realm. And then when we come together with people who are refined and intellectual, she went on, my husband drinks like a tank, acts like a chicken, tells anyone who'll listen that my grandchild makes fun of me, that the waiter makes fun of me—I'd forgotten that guy—and that my husband himself makes fun of me by twisting a story on a subject that shouldn't be a laughing matter and that nobody understands is really serious." Jean-Lino pointed out (or tried to) that several people at the party had taken her side. "No, no, no," Lydie said, "only one person, and even her—it was that ice-cold researcher lady. You saw how she looked when I said I sing. Even your darling Elisabeth, your dear friend, didn't say anything. All those people who're supposed to be in science or whatever don't give a damn. They don't worry about a thing, their brains stop at their specialty. And they're probably the people who developed the antibiotics they stick into the industrial pig farms. The crazy guy was right about that: The men stuff their bellies and their pockets too. They don't give a damn about the hideous slaughterhouses, they kill off nature and that's fine with them. And you don't care either, all you care about is going downstairs to smoke your lousy Chesterfields."

Jean-Lino doesn't know what to do. Leave her stewing and go have his smoke, or stay and try to smooth things over. She was sitting at her desk, a little antique writing table in the living room, she'd put on her glasses and was reading her emails on the laptop with the look of a woman getting back to things worth her interest. He'd never seen her do her mail at night. Making up looks like a long haul. He decides to go out and have his smoke. He puts on his biker jacket and leaves. He takes the stairs down. Reaching our floor, he hears the sound of voices. People are leaving our apartment and standing around on the landing to wait for the elevator. He thinks my sister and Serge are probably in the group. He hears laughter, hears my charming voice (the word he used). Even though the door separating the stairwell from the landing is closed, he moves back up a few steps to avoid being seen. He has lost all confidence. He's ashamed. An hour earlier he'd been part of that merry band, he'd felt included, maybe even appreciated at certain points. Now he doesn't even want to risk running into any of them downstairs. Even when these people have left, others might still come along. When he hears the elevator set off and our apartment door close, he climbs back up to the fifth floor. He sits down on the highest step, on the worn carpeting, and lights his cigarette. It's the first time he's smoked in the stairwell. He'd never thought of it before. He thinks back over the evening. He smiles as he reviews the good moments, he didn't feel the mockery when he was making people laugh, but maybe he's naïve. He and Lydie—they aren't used to going out, at least not to this sort of gathering. At the beginning, they'd been a little shy, but they'd soon felt comfortable. He's no longer sure of anything. All he knows is that he was happy and now he isn't. And that somebody did something that deprived him of his high spirits. I understood him better than anyone, he'd found somebody to talk to. My father didn't know how to lose his temper without hitting. At dinner once when I was feeling cheerful, I spiked up a potato from the platter with a knife and stuck the thing whole into my mouth. I got a smack instantly and I still feel the scorch of it today. Not because he'd hit me—I was used to that—but because he had shot down my high spirits. Jean-Lino has a sense of some injustice. He sees himself, doubled over on the top step in his leather jacket, in the horrid light of the stairwell. Lydie's words about Rémi come back to him. He had managed to avoid hearing them too well; he'd had a few drinks and that helped. But everything was gone, vanished—the pleasure, the euphoria. Did the boy despise him? Jean-Lino didn't believe a child that age could feel such a sentiment, but she'd also said he knew nothing about children. He'd given up on *Grampa Lino*, was hoping for something else, something more substantial and deeper. The last time he saw Rémi, he'd taken him to the zoo with its amusement park. It was a weekday, during the school winter break. On the Metro he'd bought the boy a laser pen from a hawker. The ride was long, with changes. After tracing zigzags on the floor and the walls, Rémi had begun attacking the passengers with his ray pen. Jean-Lino told him to aim just at the feet but he raised the beam surreptitiously to people's faces while pretending to be looking elsewhere. People yelled and Jean-Lino had to confiscate the toy until the zoo stop. Rémi sulked. Even when they reached the park he lagged behind. He brightened at the trick mirrors, breaking up over the distorted shapes they made of his body and especially of Jean-Lino's. They went on the Enchanted River trip, the bumper cars, the Russian Mountains, the place wasn't crowded and they could do it all with no waiting. Rémi flew the airplanes, at the game booths they won a plush monkey, a water pistol, a bubble blower, a boomerang ball, Rémi ate a chocolate crêpe and they shared a cone of cotton candy. Rémi wanted to ride a dromedary—he'd seen that in a picture at the entry gate—and they looked for the animals but there were none; they'd be back in the springtime, like the ponies, they were told. Again Rémi sulked. They went to the playground. Jean-Lino sat down on a bench. Rémi too. Jean-Lino asked if he'd like to climb the giant spiderweb. Rémi said no. He burrowed his head into his parka hood, leaving his new toys scattered about him as if he'd stopped caring about them. Jean-Lino said he'd finish his cigarette and then they'd leave. A boy Rémi's age walked past them, playing railroad train and marking a track in the sand ahead of him with a branch. Rémi gazed after him. The kid came past again and stopped. He pointed to their bench and said, That there is the Maleficia Station.

Rémi asked where he'd gotten the branch, they went off together to a little clump of bushes. Two minutes later they tore past Jean-Lino; Rémi had become a train. After several circuits they abandoned their branches and climbed into the toboggan slide from the bottom. They emerged giggling from the top, knocking over the little kids who'd just come up the ladder. They did all sorts of things around the playground, they dug through the sand down to the concrete, they conferred awhile leaning against the doorpost of a wooden hut, they climbed around the giant spiderweb and played at hanging dangerously from it. Rémi was livelier than Jean-Lino had ever seen him. Even from a distance, he could feel the boy's overexcitement, the urgent complicity with the new friend. He also saw Rémi's desire to conform, his submission. Jean-Lino felt cold. He made occasional signals to the boy, who didn't see them. He was tired of waiting there on the hard bench. Dusk was coming on. And he was feeling something he couldn't admit to—a sense of abandonment. As he thought back on that afternoon in the park now, alone in the service stairwell, melancholy gripped him again. He remembered the toys he'd had to go around picking up and stuffing into a cotton sack he bought at a kiosk. Rémi had refused to carry it, and Jean-Lino had slung it across his own back and lugged it home himself. Aside from the bubble blower, the other toys had never come out of the bag since. In the Metro, Rémi had fallen asleep against his shoulder, and had put a hand into his as they crossed streets on the way home. Lydie's words darken those pictures. He doesn't know what to think anymore. The words have seeped into his body and are bleeding him uncontrollably. Jean-Lino crushes out his cigarette on the concrete step, he slips the stub beneath the carpet. His feet look skinny in his dress loafers. He feels small—in size, in everything.

Some days, when I wake up, my age hits me smack in the face. Our youth is dead. We'll never be young again. It's that "never again" that's dizzying. Yesterday I reproached Pierre for being soft, easily satisfied with little. I finally said, "You let life just go by." He cited a colleague, an econ professor who'd died of a heart attack a month earlier, he said Max gobbled up life, one project after another, look what it got him. That makes me a little blue, it's hard to keep projecting forward. But maybe the very idea of the future is destructive. There are languages that don't even have a future tense.

The Americans has become my bedside book. Ever since I opened it again, I leaf through it a little every day. In Savannah an afternoon in 1955, which is the year all the photos in the book were taken, a couple is crossing a street. He is a soldier in uniform, shirt and peaked cap. He might be about fifty, pipe in his jaw, relaxed in that

American way, despite his pudgy body and the potbelly sliced at the middle by his waistband. The woman is much shorter even in heels and she's holding onto his arm in the old-fashioned way, by the crook at his elbow. Robert Frank has caught them full front, both looking into the lens. She is well turned out, molded into a dark pretty dress trimmed at the pockets and neck, with patent-leather pumps. She's smiling at the photographer. She looks older than the man, a face lined with difficulties, anyhow that's what I see. You think right off that it's not every day she goes strolling on a man's arm, that she's having a day of splendor with her new handbag, her girlish hairdo, her strapping fella in his officer's cap. It was a Sunday of life like you get sometimes, when good luck befalls you. The first time I saw Lydie, she was crossing the lobby and leaving the building on Jean-Lino's arm. In mid-afternoon, she too dressed to the nines, all done up and head high, proud of herself, of her life, of her little pockmarked man. They had just moved in. Maybe she never walked out that door again with the same radiant satisfaction. We all do that at some point, man or woman—strut out on somebody's arm as if we were the only one in the world to have hit the jackpot. We ought to hold onto such flashes of glory. We can't hope for anything in life to last. I talked to Jeanne on the phone: her adventure is losing steam. The picture-framer is less and less eager and more and more dissolute. When our mother died Jeanne tried to use the sad event to bring a touch of sentiment into the relationship. The boyfriend made clear he didn't much care and sent her a lot of hard-core messages as the days passed—he wants to drag her to orgies and offer her to other men, etc. When she resists, he turns aggressive. Jeanne calls me almost every day, half-crying. She tells me, "He puts these pictures in my head, now I feel like I want to go and see. But I'm not up to it. I'm vulnerable. I'm alone. I have no railing to hold onto, to take a slide into hell you need a railing, I slide down and I stay at the bottom."

Jean-Lino opens the door back into the apartment. He takes off his biker jacket and hangs it up in the vestibule. Lydie is still at her desk and the computer. Jean-Lino walks into the living room. She's wearing her tortoise-shell butterfly glasses low on her nose and she doesn't turn her head. He'd like to make her understand that a radical change has occurred, and to say something definitive. But he's frail, his mind is muddled.

Nothing comes to him. On the glass-topped bar, alongside the bottles, he sees the Spider-Man bubble blower from the zoo. Rémi loved to blow bubbles on the balcony. When there was a wind, he would rush to see whether they'd floated around the building and past his little corner room. Before dinner the day they'd come back from the park, he had crouched down between the plants at the base of the balustrade, with his nose stuck between the rails. He's a real professional, he can make giant bubbles, tiny ones in clusters, some that look *pregnant* one inside another, weird shapes he calls "Bizarroids." After a while there was no more fluid in the jar. Jean-Lino refilled it with a mixture of dish-washing liquid and water. He put in too much soap. The bubbles came out heavy, and they stung the skin. Rémi poured the whole jar down onto the heads of passersby. The people shouted up. Rémi hid, giggling. Jean-Lino laughed too. Lydie rushed over to close the window to the balcony, asking him why he was doing such a thing at his age. Rémi said he'd emptied the jar because the stuff Jean-Lino made hurt his skin and his eyes. Lydie yelled at Jean-Lino. The boy waited for that to be over with no expression. Jean-Lino remembers that impassive look. At the time he'd taken it for discomfort, the embarrassment children feel when grownups squabble. But maybe it was something worse—indifference, disdain? Lydie's words eat at him. Her hair is the same color as the lampshade. He thinks she looks like a fortune-teller. She's holding herself super-erect, he can feel her hostility from the small of her back to her shoulder blades. Jean-Lino pours himself a glass of Fernet-Branca and drinks it standing stolidly in the center of the living room. For a second, the idea crosses his mind to pick up the lamp and slam it down on her head. Lydie is busy with the screen. She takes notes on a pad alongside. Jean-Lino goes over to see. She's on some farm-animal protection site, he can make out a text on the agony of turkeys. He slams down the lid of the computer and says, "You drive us nuts with your barnyard, I'm sick of all that." She tries to raise the lid but he's pressing his hand down on it. She says, with a scornful snigger, "I know you don't give a damn about it."

"Yes, absolutely," Jean-Lino says, "I don't give a damn in hell about the chicken, the turkey, the pigs, about all those animal-rights people, I don't give a shit about the life the chicken leads, I'm glad to eat your organic chicken because it tastes better but apart from that I don't give a damn, I don't care if it had a miserable life, what do we know about it, I don't care if it never saw daylight, never hopped around in the trees like a damn blackbird or if it rolled in the dirt, I don't believe chickens have conscious-ness, chickens are made to be raised and killed and eaten. Now come to bed."

She tries to resist but he stands in front of her across the table. He's neither sturdy nor large but he's still stronger than she is. She finally drops the struggle. Pushing back her chair to head for the bedroom, she says, "That's the real you."

"That's the real me, yes! Yes, yes, that's me! I'm glad you're finally seeing it! And you think you were honoring me when you had the nerve to ask in that sweet-sour voice of yours where that lady got the chicken for her pâté, when you said you 'don't eat chicken unless you know where it came from' as if we were in some cheap Chinese and it might be rat meat! You could have just not eaten it yourself, but no, you had to raise the subject, had to get on your high horse and teach people a moral lesson, so everyone should know about your virtuous behavior."

He follows her to the bedroom. She tries to keep him out. Not possible. She sits on the bed and starts to take the barrettes out of her hair. She does it with meticulous attention, setting them one by one into a pouch, the activity pointedly barring any other concern.

"I'm sick of these constant rules," Jean-Lino goes on, exasperated by this maniacal concentration, "sick of living in terror, if I feel like eating chicken every day I'll eat it every day, there are people like you who won't eat anything but grains and greens, there are more and more people like you, so eat your damn greens all of you and quit pissing us off."

"Leave my room."

"It's my room too."

"You're dead drunk."

"What I don't understand is a person having the time to feel pity for all that stuff. OK, pity, but at least pity people. The world is horrible. Folks are dying on our doorstep and you guys are pitying chickens. There's a limit to pitying. You can't do it about everything or you're like Abbé Pierre, incidentally he was a bastard, he'd be pitying street bums and spit on the Jews. Even him, he didn't have a big enough heart."

"You know what separates us from animals?" Lydie shouts. "You know how much distance there is between us and animals? This much!" She snaps her fingers. "And it gets smaller every day! Ask your scientist friends!"

"We know all about your theories."

"They're not mine!"

"Yeah, make that disgusted look, purse your lips, go ahead, do all your harpy faces, go ahead."

"Leave the room, Jean-Lino."

"I belong here."

"I want to be alone."

"Go in the other room."

"Tell that cat to get out of the room."

"No, he belongs here too."

"He doesn't belong in my bedroom!"

"Be nice to him a little, he's sad all alone."

"We've already had this discussion."

"The poor thing. How come you don't feel pity for him, since you care so much about animal welfare?"

"Fuori Eduardo!"

"You shouldn't yell at him."

"Out, asshole!"

The cat looks at Lydie haughtily and doesn't budge. Lydie sticks out a leg and shoves him hard. The sharp heel of the Gigi Dool pump hits Eduardo in the side. He yelps in pain. By Jean-Lino's own account, the howl shocks them both, but it's too late. At the instant Lydie leans toward the cat, Jean-Lino grabs her by the hank of hair loosed from the barrettes and twists her neck back. She tries to turn to free herself but he no longer knows what he's doing, he clutches the tufts of hair in both hands and wrenches them in opposite directions. She's frightened. She looks ugly to him. From her distorted mouth comes no intelligible word, only shrill sounds that irritate him. Jean-Lino wants silence. He wants that throat to stop producing sounds. He squeezes the neck. Lydie struggles, rears up. He's had too much to drink. He is insane. No knowing.

He presses the neck, pressing with his thumbs, he wants her to give in, to lie still, he squeezes until nothing moves.

It takes him some time to understand what just happened. At first he thinks that, considering Lydie's personality, she's pretending to be dead. She's faked a faint or a seizure in the past. He shakes her gently. He says her name. He tells her to quit playing games. He lets a moment go by in total silence so Lydie will think he's left the room. Eduardo plays along, sitting completely motionless the way feral cats can do.

Lydie persists in her stillness. It's her eyes that alert him. They are open. He doesn't think it's possible for a person to sustain that stare of unvarying stupor. The idea of death crosses his mind. Lydie might be dead. He puts a finger beneath her nostrils. He feels nothing. Neither warmth nor breath. But really, he didn't press hard. He leans close to her face. He hears nothing. He pinches a cheek, he lifts a hand. He carries out these gestures with terror and timidity. The tears come. He collapses.

He told me: I collapsed onto her body and I cried. The mouth tic was back in force. A thrust forward of the whole jaw to shape a U with the lower lip. The night was still pitch dark, I could see through the window. From that apartment the kitchen window gives onto empty sky. I wondered if Lydie was floating there somewhere (and watching us through the glass). From time to time that old worry comes back to me—that the dead see us. After she died, my father's sister came back and broke the ceiling light in our living room. We knew it was her because they'd promised each other whichever of them died first would break something in the other one's house to prove survival in the afterlife. Aunt Micheline had raised her head and said, I'll get me one of those tulips up there. The night she was buried, an opaline shade from the chandelier fell and smashed on the table for no reason. Goddamn that's Aunt Micheline there! But where is she? Jeanne and I asked. They're here, they see everything, my mother said. After which, all my illicit activities were ruined by Aunt Micheline's all-seeing eye. Wherever I took cover, there she was. A middle-school friend and I used to go off into the bushes to show and touch each other's pussy. My aunt would be watching in horror. Not a thicket in the world could shield me from Aunt Micheline. My father too—I thought he must be prowling around somewhere. But by then I was a grownup, that didn't bother me anymore. He'd mellowed in his last years. There was something unfinished about him. He died just before I got my biology doctorate. I was glad to know he was seeing that. I even lifted the bound dissertation up real high so he could look it over.

I said, "Jean-Lino, what did you want to do with Lydie's body?"

"Take it to her office."

"Is that far?"

"Rue Jean-Rostand. A couple of minutes by car."

"Her therapy office?"

"Yes. She lived there before we got this place."

Silence.

"But when you got there, what would you do?"

"There's an elevator."

"You'd put her inside?"

"Yes."

"By yourself?"

"The studio's only one flight up. I'd have time to get up there ahead."

"She would have been strangled there in her office?"

"Somebody could have followed her in from the street ..." Silence. He strides the flat with a few wild swings of his arms.

"She would have gone to her office in the middle of the night? After the party?"

"We'd have had a fight, she'd have left the apartment. She's done it before."

"To sleep there?"

"Yes. But she came back."

The expression upset us. He'd said it that way without thinking. My mother on her bed had suddenly gone flat and she looked like a bird that had been shot. We don't believe in any metamorphosis for a bird. For birds we don't imagine some final migration. We accept the nothingness. I stood up, I went to look out at the Deuil-l'Alouette night outside the window. Not much to see—streetlamps, rooftops, building shadows, half-naked trees. An insignificant stage set, a scene that could easily be swept away in two seconds. I thought about Pierre, that he'd abandoned us. I turned around and I said, "Shall we do it?"

"Do what?"

"Take Lydie to her office?"

"I don't want to get you involved ..."

"We take her down, I help you put her into the car, and I disappear."

"No ..."

"There's no time to discuss it. It's now or never."

"You take the elevator down and that's all."

"You won't be able to put her into the car by yourself. You have the suitcase?"

He stood up, I followed him into the little room where Rémi probably slept and that in our flat had been Emmanuel's. He turned on the ceiling light; it spread a bluish glow. The bed was covered with all sorts of toys. From a closet Jean-Lino pulled a hard-sided valise, an imitation Samsonite. I said, "You don't have anything bigger?"

"No."

"She'll never fit in that."

"It holds a lot."

"Open it up."

He set the bag on the floor and opened it. I stepped into it, I tried sitting, but I couldn't manage to double over even halfway. "You're a lot bigger."

"This is the only one you have?"

"I think Lydie could fit."

"No! She could not! . . ."

I took the suitcase and we went into the bedroom. Lydie was still the same, stretched out with her scarf. We opened the valise again, in a glance it was clear she wouldn't fit into it. I thought of our big red canvas bag down in the basement. "I have one that might work," I said.

Jean-Lino shook his head, looking distraught. He was annoying me a little. No initiative. "Shall I go get it?"

"I can't let you do that."

"The problem is, it's in the basement, and the key is in my apartment."

"No, Elisabeth, let it go."

"I'll try. If Pierre's asleep, that'll work."

I took the stairs down to my place. I opened the front door quietly. Without turning on the lights, I went to see whether Pierre was still sleeping. He was sleeping and snoring. I closed the bedroom door. In the vestibule, I opened the drawer where we keep the keys. I felt around. The basement keys were not there. Without panicking I thought for a moment. I remembered going down there that day to get the stool. I'd been wearing a cardigan with pockets. The cardigan was in the bedroom. I went back there, I snatched the cardigan that was hanging on a chair, being careful not to let the keys fall out. I dashed down the stairs. Our own storage unit is at the end of a corridor. The floor to it is partly unpaved. It bothered me to walk on it with my fur slippers, I walked the rest on tiptoe. I emptied the big suitcase of a smaller one and a few bags that were inside. As I made my way back along the corridor, the timed lights went out. I didn't turn them back on. I climbed the steep stairs blind. I edged open the door to the lobby. Empty and unlit. The elevator was there and I took it back up to Jean-Lino's floor. The apartment door was open. The whole thing done at the speed of a pro. I was rather proud of my cool.

The red canvas suitcase lay open at the foot of Lydie's bed. Jean-Lino had put theirs away. The red one was wider, suppler. The plan seemed feasible. On the night table burned a decorative candle he must have lit while I was downstairs. The two of us stood there without speaking. Again Jean-Lino's arms were dangling loose and his neck was ducked forward. What were we waiting for?! After a moment he said, "Are you Catholic, Elisabeth?"

"I'm not anything."

He opened his hand. He was holding a thin chain with a golden medal of the Virgin.

"I'd like to put this on her."

"Go ahead."

"I can't open the catch."

"Give it to me."

Some links of the chain had got tangled around the hook.

"This will take hours," I said.

He snatched the necklace out of my hands and began laboring over it with unpracticed fingers.

"We don't have the time for that, Jean-Lino."

He was no longer listening. He fussed with the chain, his hands a half inch in front of his glasses, clawed like a crustacean's, his mouth tight with hatred.

"What the hell are you doing, Jean-Lino?"

He seemed beside himself. I tried to pry his hands open, I wound up slapping him.

"I'd like to do something!"

"What is it you want to do?"

"Some ritual . . ."

"What kind of ritual? You already lit a candle, that's very good."

"I said the beginning of the *Shema.*"

"What's that?"

"The Jewish prayer."

"Fine."

"But Lydie is Catholic."

"First I've heard."

"She had other beliefs too, but she was firm about staying Catholic."

"So make the sign of the cross!"

"I don't know how."

"OK, OK, let's put her in the suitcase, Jean-Lino!!"

"Yes, I'm talking nonsense."

I took up a position by the feet. Jean-Lino slipped his arms beneath Lydie's shoulders. He said, "Got to double her over first and then slide her in." I was glad to see him get back to technical style right away. I'd never manipulated a dead body. Touched one, kissed one, yes. Manipulated, no. She wasn't wearing tights, the contact with her skin startled me with its tepid temperature. We easily turned her onto her side. She half-rolled onto her belly, stretched out long as if she were mocking us. Before shifting her into the valise we'd have to fold her up. I sensed that Jean-Lino wanted to handle the job by himself. He circled the suitcase, he lifted the thighs through the skirt and drew them to the front so the knees bent. Next he grasped the waist so that would fold too. He finished by curling the upper body. All done with swiftness and delicacy. Lydie politely let it happen, with her kerchief and her tranquil countrywoman face. In the end she looked like a little girl asleep on the bed in the fetal position. I felt that Jean-Lino was uneasy about tipping her in. I offered a hand, thinking to hold her back and avoid a rough drop into the suitcase. She got there rumpled and askew. We had to rearrange her and tuck in whatever stuck out. The look of childlike serenity was gone. Lydie was compressed, contorted. Her curly hair bulged out of the scarf in a strange clump against the red lining.

We'd had to take off her shoes and jam them into the interstices. I could see that Jean-Lino was suffering. I took it on myself to work the zipper closed. But buckling the straps required pressing down and sitting on top of the suitcase. I did sit on it. I felt the soft bulk of the body give way beneath my buttocks. I said "Help me." He took up the other buckle strap and pulled.

"This is awful."

"She's dead, Jean-Lino, she doesn't feel anything."

It didn't close. There was still a gap on one side. Jean-Lino sat too. I stood up to drop on my rear as heavily as possible. Jean-Lino did the same, we stood and we dropped, gaining a quarter inch or two of zipper each time. Finally I lay full length on the thing, Jean-Lino lay in the opposite direction, both of us squirming on the bulges like rolling pins on a crust. When the tab had swallowed up the last few teeth, we were exhausted. Jean-Lino got up before I did. He slapped down and smoothed his hair ten times in a row. Now the purse and the coat, he said, fitting his glasses back on. I followed him into the living room. Lydie's bag sat on the floor, wide open, next to the desk. I took a quick look at the notepad beside the computer. I made out the words *ulcers, cannibalism*, then the figure *25,000*, then an arrow and the words, underlined, *Life and death of a bird. Procedures like Frankenstein's. Suffering imprinted into their (very) genes.* The pen lay across the page. The lamp, with its saffron shade, was lit. I'd never seen her handwriting. Those words, slightly slanted, a memo, gave me a sharper sense of Lydie's existence than any moment of her physical presence ever had. The act of noting, the words themselves, and the unknown person they were meant for. And more mysteriously, the word *bird*. The word *bird* applied to poultry. Jean-Lino, in a crouch, was checking the contents of the purse. He took the cellphone from the table and put it into the bag. Eduardo came over and looked inside too. A terrible anguish gripped me. I no longer understood what we were doing. I saw myself a few hours earlier in that same spot, a chair in one hand, signing the petition against grinding up baby chicks. Lydie Gumbiner opening drawers to find things to lend me. The brevity of the passage from life to death felt dizzying. A bagatelle.

Jean-Lino opened a closet, he took out the green coat I knew well—a long Russian redingote style, tight through the waist and flared below. I used to see her from my window trotting through the parking lot in that coat and short boots. Every winter, I'd see the redingote reappear, it marked the flow of time for me in Deuil-l'Alouette. I'd worn an ankle-length coat myself back in that maxi period. I'd never got completely into the style. One day, on an escalator in the Galeries Lafayette, the hem had caught between two steps. The machinery jammed and made the thing stop short. I waited there in my coat for someone to come and free me; it never occurred to me to slip out of it. Jean-Lino went back into the bedroom. I heard a collision, then the sound of wheels in the small hallway. I saw my red valise in the doorway. Swollen, monstrous, the telescoping handle raised to its highest position.

⌒

When you ask Etienne for news on his eyesight, he answers, *It's all under control*. It's an expression he got from his father who was a police chief. I've always heard him say that—"it's under control"—even when nothing is working. And actually his vision is not at all under control, since what he's got is the dry macular degeneration, the bad kind, the form that, unlike the wet, is not helped by the shots. We don't often ask Etienne for news on his vision. We don't want that to become a topic of conversation. On the other hand, we can't never worry about it. It's a subtle balance between reserve and intrusion. On his own in the house last weekend, Etienne thought he could adjust the thermostat by touch, without his glasses or a flashlight. He turned the dial in the wrong direction. When Merle came back, she walked into a white-hot oven. "All under control" has the virtue of closing the chapter that's barely opened. The line says nothing about reality, nor even about the speaker's state of mind. It's a rather practical kind of existential readiness—a standing to attention. And funny too. The body does whatever it chooses, the cells behave any way they want. In the end, what's serious?

Recently we were talking about an episode from the time when their older son was still in high school. Merle and Etienne had got a notice from the headmaster saying that Paul Dienesmann had behaved very badly at Auschwitz. Etienne called his son into his study and, seated and looking grave, said to him—we still laugh about it—"It seems you behaved very badly at Auschwitz?" Further discussion revealed that Paul had been clowning on the bus that drove the class from Krakow to Birkenau, creating among his classmates an atmosphere antithetical to Remembrance and Contemplation. I've taken a dislike to the word "contemplation." And to the principle as well. It's become a huge fashion ever since the world has been heading into indescribable chaos. Politicians and citizens (another brilliantly empty word) spend their time "contemplating." I liked it better before, when you carried your enemy's head around on a pike. Even virtue isn't serious. This morning, before I left for the Pasteur, I phoned the retirement home to ask after Jean-Lino's aunt. With the conversation finished, I think, You're really a good person, you're concerned for others. Two seconds later I tell myself, It's disgusting, this self-satisfaction over such an elementary deed. And immediately after that, Good, you keep a firm eye on your own motives, bravo. There's always some great congratulator who has the last word. When Denner, as a child, came out of confession, he used to stop in front of Saint Joseph, breathe deep, and say to himself, Now I'm a saint. And right afterward, going down the stairs: Oh shit—sin of pride. One way or another, virtue doesn't last. It can only exist if we're not aware of it. I miss Denner. A man dead thirty years ago you suddenly miss. A person who would know nothing about my life, or my work, or husband or child, where I live, the places I've seen, or what I looked like over time. Or a million other things unimaginable back then. If he came by now what a laugh we'd have! About everything. Is there, somewhere up in the sky, a little Denner star? Seems to me I catch sight of it now and then. Joseph Denner was four years older than me. Big, muscular, anarcho and alky. His father was a line cook; at fourteen he'd been a dishwasher at the Colmar railroad station. I know that still because Denner always talked about it. Joseph had loved and admired his father, but not his mother, according to him she was a stingy petit-bourgeois monster. They lived in three connected maid's rooms on the rue Legendre, the bathroom was also the kitchen and they'd cover the tub with a lid for a work surface. I remember a tiny slope-ceilinged living room area. And behind it, set off by a gilded metal gate that was always shut, the parents' bedroom, also tiny. The liquor was in a cupboard back there. The top of the gate was a twisted scroll section with an opening in it. By some supernatural writhing Denner would slither through it sideways to get us some whiskey. He'd done two years' military service in Germany with a disciplinary battalion. To scrape by he played guitar in the Pax Quartet, a more or less Catholic band that kept him on out of kindness. He believed in adventure, we dreamed of mountain climbing, about Machu Picchu, while we slugged down Carlsbergs in the Miquel Pub, we never went anywhere except for a few nighttime spins up to the seaside. He was thin-skinned and volatile. We were all younger than him, nobody dared to contradict him. I still have some books that belonged to him, Vian, Genet, Buzzati. He adored them. I've always kept them separate, in a corner, wherever I live, alongside the photography books, the little collection the two of us put together—Frank, Kertész, Cartier-Bresson, Winogrand, Weegee, Weiss, Arbus (we swiped them from the Pereire bookstore; at some surplus outlet Denner had found a hunting vest with a big pocket in the back). In certain Garry Winogrand photos the girls come out in the street in hair curlers with scarves wrapped around them. That gives them a slutty, don't-give-a-damn look, really sexy. I did it for a while myself. I've always been interested in what people do with hair. You can't conceive of the world, or even of people in general. You can only conceive of things you've touched. All great events nourish thought and mind, like theater. But it's not the great events or great ideas that make for life, it's ordinary things. The only things I've retained inside me, truly, are things close by, things I could touch with my hands. Everything's under control.

—

"... Jean-Lino?" The suitcase had got as far as the vestibule by itself. Silence. I went to look. Jean-Lino was standing in the hallway, a bit like a shadow puppet silhouetted in the light from the bedroom. "You OK?"

"Elisabeth."

"You're scaring me."

"In case something should happen to me, you never came back up here to my place. You don't know anything."

"All right."

"And the suitcase is mine."

"All right."

He put on his Zara biker jacket and his racetrack hat. He set the purse and the coat on top of the suitcase.

"The robber would certainly have taken the wallet . . ."

"Yes. I'll get rid of it . . . Ah, just a second . . ." He went into the bedroom again and came back with a pair of fleece-lined gloves. "Let's go."

We left the apartment. Jean-Lino pulled the load. We stood still for a few seconds on the landing to be sure we heard nothing. I pressed the elevator button. Actually it was still at his floor. We pushed the suitcase inside. Jean-Lino opened the door to the service stairs. Not a sound. We agreed in whispers that I would wait a moment to go down so we would reach the lobby at the same time. He turned on the hall lights and disappeared into the stairwell. I stepped into the elevator, leaving the door ajar. The cabin is very small, there wasn't much room left. The green coat fell to the floor, I picked it up and pushed it between the vertical bars of the raised handle. I tried to fit the handle through the straps of the handbag but that didn't work. I let the door close and pressed the lobby button. I looked at my feet, my checkered pajama pants, my fake-fur slippers. I was going down four stories alone with a corpse. No panic. I felt super-daring, really proud. I told myself, You would have been great in the Underground or spying for the Foreign Service. Look at you, Elisabeth! Ground floor. Jean-Lino was already there. Breathless and focused. Him too—terrific. He took the suitcase. The coat fell to the floor again, I picked it up. I was carrying the purse and the coat. The wheels made an upsetting noise on the tile floor. The car was parked out front. I could see it just past the stone curb. I calculated the trip, going around the shrubs. I pressed the door button. Jean-Lino opened it. He pulled the suitcase into the half-open doorway. A motor started up behind the building. We heard a small sound coming from outside, a damp sound of heels on wet ground, and we saw coming from the right, her head lowered against the wind, the girl from the second floor on her way home from a party. Jean-Lino drew back, he stood aside to let her come in. The girl said hello, we answered hello. She darted into the waiting elevator.

—

What could that bitch have noticed? Everything. The tall beanpole lady from the fourth floor holding a coat and a purse, in fur slippers and Hello Kitty pajamas, with the guy from the fifth floor in a fedora and gloves pulling an enormous red suitcase. Heading out for god knows where at three in the morning. Everything. At the moment he runs into the girl Jean-Lino tries to look as if there's nothing unusual going on, as if this run-of-the-mill encounter doesn't affect him. After pulling aside to let her pass, he again tugs the suitcase toward the exit.

He's already gone five yards outside when I clutch at him. "She saw us!"

"What did she see?"

"Us! With the suitcase!!"

"A person has the right to go out with a suitcase."

It's sprinkling again. An odious drizzle.

"Not tonight. A night like this people are supposed to stay home."

I can tell I'm irritating him. He tries to get the suitcase moving again by little tugs but I hold onto it.

"Who's going to ask her anything?"

"The cops!"

"Why would they come talk to her?"

I tie the coat through the tall handle again and pull at the suitcase to take it back indoors. He blocks it.

"Because there'll be an investigation! They'll question the neighbors."

"Go home, Elisabeth. I'll manage."

"She saw me, too. Our plan is ruined!"

"So what do we do?" He is frantic.

"Well at least let's go back inside."

"She fucked up the whole thing, that bitch!" He is shouting. He's losing it. "I'm gonna kill her!"

"Jean-Lino, let's go back . . ."

He lets go. I grab the retractable handle and drag the suitcase. The coat slides down, the case rolls over it and brakes, stopping me short and almost tripping me. That damn coat, falling down every two minutes!! Back into the lobby. The coat is a mess. Everything's wet. Jean-Lino, with nothing in his gloved hands now, looks like he's disguised as a fur trapper. He pulls a flattened cigarette pack from his jacket and lights up. He says, "What the hell was she doing out so late, the slut?"

"We can't just stay here."

"I'm gonna shut her mouth, that bitch."

"Let's go into the stairwell and think."

I pulled the suitcase toward the far wall and stood it in the corner beside the service door. "Come on into the stairwell, Jean-Lino."

I caught his arm by the leather of the jacket and I pushed him toward the stairs. He let it happen for two or three steps, his legs stiff like a robot's. I sat down on the lowest stairs at the spot where he'd broken down in front of Rémi. Jean-Lino drew the smoke in deep with that mouth action of his, staring at the suitcase. After a moment he moved toward it, unsteadily. He stroked its top with his sheepskin glove. From left to right, several times in sequence like an unspoken poem. Then he slipped to his knees, moaning. His widespread arms gripped the case from both sides, his cheek was pressed to the canvas. He formed, half in the air, some distorted kisses. We were separated by the doorjamb—the image took on its full effect from that framing. Abyss and nonsense—why had there been no hand, no intervention, to stop the girl? Just a small flick of the thumb from the heavens to throw off by a minute her exit from the party, from the car, just one extra bit of talk there? Instead of abandoning, in this cold lobby, Jean-Lino Manoscrivi, the gentlest of men, and Lydie Gumbiner, small and crumpled in her party clothes. People who think there's some orderly system to life—they're lucky.

I was cold. I spread the green coat over my legs. Jean-Lino had let go of the suitcase. He was still on the floor with his legs folded under him, head low and hands on the nape of his neck. I waited. Then I went to get him. I moved to raise him up by encircling his shoulders. I picked up the hat and the glasses that had fallen onto the tile floor. Together we headed back toward the stairs, we sat down where I had been—that is, two yards farther along. Jean-Lino immediately stood up again to bring the suitcase in with us, it just cleared the doorframe and filled the whole space at the bottom of the stairs. The three of us were crammed tight. I'd rearranged the coat over us for protection. The situation reminded me of the huts you make as a kid. You pull everything close, the roof, the floor, the ceiling, walls, objects, bodies, you want the space to be as constricted as possible. The outer world is no longer visible except through a slit while tempest and storm rage outside.

He needed to piss. That was the first thing he said—"I have to piss."

"Go outdoors."

He didn't move.

"I drank too much. I behaved like such an ass."

"Go ahead, Jean-Lino, I'll stay here."

The light went off. We were left in near darkness. I turned it back on. I'd never seen the lobby by this glow, nor in detail. The grille on the air vent, the dirty baseboard molding. A dingy purgatory. In some book Bill Bryson said, "No room has fallen further in history than the hall." Jean-Lino did go out, I don't know where, while I stayed with the suitcase. I slipped into the coat, which was far too narrow for me, the sleeves reached only halfway down my arms and I couldn't button it. It was roughly the same color as the carpeting. I thought about what to do: Go upstairs and put Lydie back on the bed as if nothing had happened? Take the suitcase and go to my own apartment while Jean-Lino called the police? It was useless. The girl from the second floor had seen us together. Whatever there might be in the suitcase, Jean-Lino had left his house after strangling his wife and I was mixed up in the business. I reviewed the sequence of events: Jean-Lino came down to our apartment. He informed us of the catastrophe. We didn't believe him. Pierre and I went upstairs to see Lydie's body. Pierre made me go back home and not get involved. Jean-Lino had killed his wife. We had nothing to do with it. He was supposed to phone the police and turn himself in. Pierre went to sleep. I went back upstairs. And what if I hadn't gone up? What if, instead of going up, I had stayed home, full of anxiety (and curiosity), watching through the windows and the peephole for the slightest movement? Why through the peephole? For fear of some crazy reaction from Jean-Lino Manoscrivi? No. No. Just very simply because I didn't stay glued to the window. I looked through the peephole from time to time, in case I'd missed something outside.

And that's how... And that's how it happened that I saw the elevator light blinking. I opened the door, I heard the sound of someone running down the stairs. I called out to my friend Jean-Lino. I grabbed my keys and I rushed down the stairs myself. I got to the bottom just as he was heading for the front door with a huge red suitcase... I begged him not to do this stupid thing. The second-floor neighbor came in... After all, I was in slippers and pajamas, nothing like a person set to go out into the wet night... That story made sense. That could work. It could also work for Pierre. No. He knew the suitcase. He knew the damn suitcase intimately. In fact it was pretty much his suitcase. How to explain to Pierre what the red suitcase was doing there? Not to mention the cargo. Maybe I could have lent it to the Manoscrivis for some upcoming trip? Or to move things? Yes, that's good—I could have lent it for moving things over to the psychotherapy office. Without telling him? Well sure, I don't tell my husband about lending somebody a suitcase. Or better . . . Better: we didn't know about any of it. Jean-Lino never came downstairs to us, we never went upstairs. I'd given a party. I go downstairs to the trash-bins, and who do I see? As I'm coming back through the lobby? Jean-Lino Manoscrivi! Pulling the big red suitcase I'd lent to Lydie . . . I didn't wonder what was in the suitcase? No, Jean-Lino tells me he's putting it in the trunk of the car for the next morning. The second-floor neighbor walks in from a party. She sees us on our way out . . . Not me. I'm not going out. I'm there by coincidence, just walking my friend over to the lobby door. It's completely nothing. I just have to brief Pierre. He'll understand that it's in our interest.

~~

He came back. I heard the outside door. I recognized the sound of his walk. He sat down next to me in the nook. His scalp drenched because he'd left his hat off. The rain must be coming down hard. The comb-over hair was plastered to his forehead and crimped up at the edge. He said, "What's the drill?

"We can go back up . . ."

How could I tell him how close I was to abandoning him?

"...but that won't help because we could never explain what the two of us were doing here in the lobby."

He had taken off his gloves (the gloves were sticking out of the side pockets of the biker jacket like two ruffled ears). Doubled over on the stair, he skimmed a hand over the red canvas of the suitcase, tracing vague curves with his finger. The pitted cheeks gleamed, I thought from the rain, but he was crying. When Jean-Lino was a child, after the evening meal his father would sometimes pick up the Book of Psalms and read a passage aloud. The bookmark ribbon always opened to the same place. It never occurred to his father to move it, so he always read out the same verse, the one about exile: *By the rivers of Babylon, there we sat down and we wept, remembering Zion.* Jean-Lino remembered the book, its bronze cover, the fraying ribbon, and especially the engraving on the cover: people with slack expressions, half-naked, slumped against one another, on the banks of a warm stream, with a harp hooked onto the branch of a tree. He said he'd never made the connection between the verse and the image. When his father recited the words Jean-Lino would hear the roar of many rivers, picture the tumble and crash of driftwood logs beneath a sky of defeat. And as to sitting and weeping, for him that meant being in a condition of waiting, huddled and alone. He'd had no religious instruction. The Manoscrivis observed a few holidays with the mother's family, but that was mainly for eating stuffed carp. Jean-Lino understood nothing about the lines his father read him (neither did his father, according to him) but he liked hearing the phrases from the past. He felt he had some part in the history of mankind, even deep in the Parmentier tenement courtyard, and he likened himself to those wanderers, to those stateless exiles. What had that silly bitch from the second floor actually registered? I went over the scene again. I saw myself by the big windowed front door, behind Jean-Lino, holding the purse and the coat. Holding the purse and the coat! Holding Lydie's purse and the long flared green frockcoat that the whole neighborhood knows . . . I'd have to drop the trashbin story, go back to the previous version. Yes, I was carrying the purse and the coat. I had torn them from Jean-Lino's hands to keep him from committing an insane act. "Jean-Lino," I murmured, "we have to call the police."

"Yes."

"I have a little idea for what we can say about my being there . . ."

"Yes . . ."

I set out the story. Lending the suitcase to Lydie, his panicky arrival at our place, our visit upstairs to check the body, my lookout watch, the peephole, me imploring him in the lobby. He had no reaction, he didn't care. It made me angry that he wouldn't care about getting me out of the situation. He kills his wife, I do my best to help him, and now that it's ruined he doesn't give a damn about the whole thing. I shook him, "You listening to me, Jean-Lino? It's not about you anymore, it's about me. It's important for us to have the same version of what happened."

"Yes, it's important . . ."

He fumbles in a chest pocket, pulls out some tickets and balls of colored tinfoil. There's also a transparent square of self-stick arrows that he tosses on the floor with the rest.

"Can you repeat what I just said? What do I say when I get to the lobby and see you with all this stuff?"

"You snatch the purse and the coat away from me . . ."

"And—?"

"And you say, 'You're crazy.'"

"No, I don't say right away that you're crazy, first I say, 'What are you doing? What's in that suitcase?'"

He looks at the floor and the bits of paper. "Yes . . ."

"You listening, Jean-Lino?"

"You say, 'What's in the suitcase?' . . ."

"And then I say, 'You're crazy, don't do that!'"

"Yes yes, sure Elisabeth, I put you completely in the clear, completely . . ."

He shakes his head, the mouth tic is seriously back. Not a very reassuring sight.

"You have your cellphone with you?"

"No."

I open Lydie's carry-all bag and take her phone out. "We can use this one . . ."

"For what?"

"To call the police."

He gazes at the thing. An Android in a yellow case with a dangling ornament topped by a feather. I immediately regret my harshness. Everything's out of kilter. I wish I'd listened to Pierre, hadn't left our apartment. Jean-Lino seems completely elsewhere. He keeps silent; then, in a faint voice, he says, "I'll never see the mosquito laboratory."

"Someday, sure you will."

"When?"

"When you come back."

He shrugs. I had promised to take him to Pasteur and show him the museum, but especially the insectarium. Jean-Lino yearned to see the magical premises of knowledge. To go where life is learned about. At the Guli megastore he languished among the racks where large cold beasts were stacked: washing machines, stove hoods, ranges, freezers evoked nothing for him. He dreamed of being brought into the world of living things, dangerous things. I'd told him about the insectarium, a steamy incubator area of a few rooms underground where there lived hundreds of larvae in white basins and as many mosquitos from all over the world in containers sealed by knots of netting. A place that is half laboratory, half laundry, with everyday gadgets and a sewing machine for the netting. I had told him how the larvae are fed liquid cat food, how the adult males gobble up nothing but sweets and don't bite. On the other hand, I explained, their womenfolk do bite and every three days they gorge on the blood of some poor mouse that gets dropped into their cage. Jean-Lino exclaimed, "Not a word to Lydie!" I had made clear that the mouse was anesthetized, but he didn't listen. The fact was that Jean-Lino did not want to share the privilege of his visit into the culicines' lair.

"We should've gone before."

"We'll go."

"You won't be at Pasteur anymore by then."

"I can still go."

"I won't be alive then."

"OK, that's enough, we can't spend the whole night here. What's the police number, 17?" I had picked up Lydie's phone again. I went directly to the emergency number.

"Eduardo!" Jean-Lino cried. That had to come. No way to dodge the Eduardo question forever.

"Eduardo will be taken care of . . ."

"By who? The SPCA, no, no no, never! And he's sick besides!"

"We'll take him."

"You don't like him!"

"We'll see to him. And if he's not happy with us, we'll put him with people who will like him."

"You won't know how to take care of him!"

I set the phone down on the suitcase, I stood up and tried to extricate myself from the coat.

"What are you doing?"

"Leaving."

He stood up. "Let's go put him in your house."

The red had risen in his cheeks and his eyes bulged behind the yellow frames. I saw that there was no point arguing. "Quick, then," I said. We closed the door so the suitcase couldn't be seen (by whom, at three in the morning?) and took the stairs up two at a time. In his flat, Jean-Lino strode into the small bedroom and emerged in a minute with a canvas satchel. We went into the kitchen. He put in it a package of patties, making clear that these were not the ones that caused diarrhea; according to him the cat was, so to speak, if not exactly cured then at least past any trouble. There'd be two more days of treatment, we could skip the yeast and the anti-kidney-stone capsules but not the Revigor 200. He put the prescription slip and the vet's address into the bag. He took a Feliway diffuser from a closet and dropped it into the bag—to replace, he said as we moved into the living room, the facial pheromones and help the cat feel safe in the new environment. I was understanding only one word out of two. In the living room he collected some toys, balls and fake mice, then stood and spun slowly in place till he spotted a long wand tipped with a tail of imitation leopard fur and feathers. "He adores the fishing pole," he said as he shoved the whole thing into the sack. "He's a hunter, you've got to play with him at least three times a day," he commanded, heading back to the kitchen.

"Can you get the litter box?" I picked up the tray. Jean-Lino grabbed Eduardo, who was prowling around his legs. And suddenly I saw the table and I said, "Wait!" My cigarette was in the ashtray! My long cigarette, barely smoked! I'd seen too many episodes of *Bring in the Accused* not to spot the fatal blunder! I put the stub in my pocket and looked around to see if I hadn't left other traces. Eduardo meowed and bared his cat teeth. We went down the stairs, Jean-Lino first, me behind. I opened our door. Not a sound. I set the litter box down in the kitchen. I closed the door to the bedroom hallway. In the vestibule, Jean-Lino set down Eduardo and the traveling bag. He spotted a wall socket and immediately plugged in the Feliway diffuser. Down on all fours himself, his torso crammed into the biker jacket, he took the cat's muzzle in his hands and whispered to him, rubbing his nose against fur. I hurried him along, terrified at the idea that Pierre might emerge. For a moment I thought of changing into shoes before rejecting the idea as a fatal foolishness. As we were leaving, Jean-Lino drew from the bag a T-shirt that probably belonged to him, balled it up and set it in front of Eduardo.

We went back to the stairs. He let himself drop onto each step like a sleepwalker. He was out of juice. Reaching the

bottom, we sat back down on the same spot. I took up
Lydie's phone again and although I no longer understood
much about the situation, I said, "Jean-Lino, you have to
do it. And besides the battery is nearly dead."

"Where was I going with the suitcase? . . ."

"Nowhere! You weren't going anywhere. You don't
even know why you put her into the suitcase! You'd lost
your mind, you were having a fit of madness."

"A fit of madness . . ."

I dialed 17 and handed him the phone. A recorded voice
said, You are speaking to the Emergency Police, followed
by a little anxiety-producing message. Then it rang. It went
on ringing with no answer. Jean-Lino hung up.

"No answer."

"That's impossible. Call again."

"What do I say? . . . I killed my wife?"

"Not 'I killed my wife' just like that."

"So what should I say?"

"Give it a little form. Say I'm calling because I just did
something stupid . . ."

He calls again. The message again: Your conversation is
recorded, any misuse will be punished. An actual woman
picks up right after. "Emergency Police, I'm listening." Jean-
Lino looks at me in a panic. I sketch one of those gestures
that are supposed to calm your interlocutor. Completely
doubled over on himself, his head at knee level, Jean-Lino
says "I'm calling because I did something stupid . . ."

"What was it?" says the voice.

"I committed a murder . . ."

"Where are you located?"

"Deuil-l'Alouette."

"You know the address where you are?"

Jean-Lino answers in a low voice. The girl has him repeat the street name. She asks if the address is the same as his home. She sounds nice, and calm.

"Are you out on the public street or inside a building?"

Under her voice I can hear tapping at a keyboard.

"I'm inside the lobby."

"The lobby of your building?"

"Yes."

"Is there a digital door code?"

"I don't remember now . . ."

"Are you alone?"

Jean-Lino straightens up. Panic. I signal that he can mention me.

"No."

"Who're you with?"

Silently I mouth *neigh-bor*. "With my neighbor."

"One person?"

"Yes."

"Sir, what happened?"

"I killed my wife . . ."

"Yes . . . ?"

He turns to me. I find nothing to whisper.

"Where is she now, your wife? Is she with you right now? . . ."

He tries to answer but no sound comes out. The lower lip has begun trembling again, a continuous throbbing. It looks like a batrachian's buccal floor.

"What's your name, sir?"

"Jean-Lino Manoscrivi."

"Jean . . . Lino?"

"Yes . . ."

"Are you armed, Jean-Lino?"

"No. No, no."

"Your neighbor either?"

"No . . ."

"Have you consumed alcohol or drugs??"

"No . . ." He sees me mime the act of having a drink with friends. "A little alcohol . . ."

"Are you under treatment in connection with a psychiatric problem? . . ."

The call breaks off. Battery's dead . . . Jean-Lino stared at the dark screen. He closed the lid and extended the chain on the yellow plastic case to set the feather right. I laid my arm around his shoulders. Jean-Lino put his hat back on. We were in a corner of some railway station, waiting. With the long, too-small coat, my fake-fur slippers and the suitcase, a couple of Roma passing through. About to be sent off who knows where. He said, "That girl was nice." I said, "Yes, she was nice." And he: "What's going to happen to my aunt without me? She has nobody else."

Having nobody. The subjects in *The Americans* look like they have nobody. That's who they are. They exist at the edge of roads, of benches, of rooms, they've come looking for something they won't find. Now and then they gleam in some fleeting light. They have nobody. The Jehovah's Witness has nobody. He walks the streets with his briefcase stuffed with magazines, the briefcase gives him the look of a man and stands in for a destination. When you grow up with the idea you have nobody, you don't easily find your way back. Even if someone takes your hand and shelters you, it doesn't really happen for you. Sundays and holidays, on Parmentier Avenue, Jean-Lino's parents would send him out into the courtyard. He'd hang about, squatting on the cobblestones. He would scratch away at the furrows where weeds were sprouting. He would make things out of the watchmaker's trash. There were no other children. To have nobody is to have not even yourself. Somebody loving you provides a certificate of existence. When a person feels alone, he can't exist without some small social fable. When I was around twelve, I was waiting for love to give me back my lost identity (the one we're supposed to have had before Zeus cut us in half), but, unsure of such an eventuality, I also placed a bet on fame and honor. Since I was good at science, I imagined myself a future as a researcher: my team discovered a revolutionary treatment for epilepsy and I got an international medal, a Nobel kind of thing. Jeanne was my manager. She would sit on the pullout bed with Rosa the doll, who represented Therese Parmentolo, a kid from high school who had grand mal seizures, she'd listen to my acceptance speech and applaud from time to time. Afterward, Therese Parmentolo (also played by me) would come onstage to express her gratitude. Sometimes I wonder if everything we think we are might arise from a series of imitations and projections. Even though I haven't been a researcher, and took refuge in something with more security, I often hear that I extricated myself from my background or escaped my class. That's idiotic. All I did was save myself from insubstantiality. People telephone the Emergency Police number to talk because they have nobody else, a patrolman once told me. Those are the majority of calls to 17. There was one woman who would phone in several times a week. Before hanging up she would say, "Tell the whole crew hello for me." Joseph Denner used to play melancholy tunes on his guitar. He would do "Céline" by Hugues Aufray, he'd do the Beatles' "Eleanor Rigby," which he'd sing nearly in a monotone with his weak voice, a bad accent, without understanding all the words—*All the lonely people ... Where do they all belong* ... I was all those homeless people. Tell the whole crew hello. As if she meant something to the crew.

Jean-Lino says again, "We could have taken Rémi to the mosquitoes." He pulls out a pack of cigarettes, slides one up to his mouth. He is small, frail. His long nose tilts toward the floor, the yellow spectacles don't go with the hat. We could still laugh over that. The smoke trails along the suitcase and envelops us. It envelops the pitted skin, it envelops the thoughts, the world becomes one immense vaporous mass. We heard the sound of voices from outdoors, and knocking against the glass. I stood up. I stepped out from the service stairs. They were there. Three guys outside the lobby door. "They're here, I think," I said, and I went to open up. Three men came in, dressed more or less like Jean-Lino without the poetry. Police. They right away went to speak to Jean-Lino, who had just appeared at the back of the lobby. He had taken off his hat, he was holding it in one hand, his arm folded in an awkward position. "You're Monsieur Manoscrivi?" said one of the officers.

"Yes . . ."

"You're the one who called the Emergency Police?"

"Yes . . ."

Uniformed cops arrived on their heels. A girl and two guys, in their caps.

"You're the one who killed your wife? . . . Where is she, your wife?"

"In the suitcase . . ." He pointed to the stairwell and some of the officers went to take a look at the valise.

"Don't you move. We'll be taking you in to the station. And you too, madam."

They handcuffed us. The girl patted down my whole body and searched the pockets of Lydie's coat. There were some coins, a Kleenex, and the half-cigarette I had smoked up at Jean-Lino's. Oh my god. But no, no problem, I said to myself, you could have smoked it at the bottom of the stairs waiting for the cops. A patrolman said "Come, madam, we'll have a little talk." He took my arm and led me out of the building. I said, "Where are we going?"

"Into the squad car."

"Can I change my clothes?"

"Not for the moment, ma'am."

The girl was speaking into a walkie-talkie. I heard, "We entered the lobby, the suspect confirmed that he killed his wife. She is apparently inside a suitcase. There was another person with him. We have begun questioning the two persons. We'll need an OPJ when we get in." I asked, "Where are we being taken?"

"To the police station."

"Will we be going together?" I said, pointing to Jean-Lino.

The cop drew me along without answering.

"I'm wearing bedroom slippers!"

"Slippers are fine. At least that way you won't have to take out any shoelaces."

Jean-Lino was no longer visible among the men.

"Will I be with him over there?"

"OK, OK, time to leave now."

"Will I see him later?"

"I don't know, ma'am."

The man was losing patience. I called out, in a voice I didn't recognize, a sharp wrenching cry that emerged after an effort I was unused to and that hurt me, "Jean-Lino, see you later!" The cop turned me around, he slid a hand beneath my left arm and pushed me outside by pressing my shoulder. I thought I saw some commotion among the men at the rear of the lobby, I thought I saw Jean-Lino's face for a moment, I even thought I heard my name, but I'm not sure of anything. Supported by the man's grip, with my head lowered I walked onto the wet parking lot, my checkered pajama pants sliding down, they were too big for me but I couldn't pull them up. The police car was right out front, parked crosswise on the driveway. He had me get in through the right rear door. He came around to sit on the other side. He took out a pen and a notebook. He asked me my name, address, date and place of birth. He wrote them down carefully and slowly. On a third of the page, in white on a black square, there was the drawing of a key with the words BRUET INC.—*Locksmith and Glazier.* I said, "Who'll tell my husband?"

"We're going to take you into custody and read you your rights."

I wasn't too clear what that meant. Nor what it had to do with Pierre. But I was too tired to try to understand.

"You're connected to a locksmith business?"

"Companies give us these freebie pads to advertise."

"Oh, I see . . ."

"On actual cases, we work with some contract outfits. That doesn't stop other ones from sending stuff over all the time."

"What does a glazier do for you?"

"Nothing. The companies do both kinds of things. They give us pens and calendars too . . . the calendars are a good deal because they work as stationery too. It's smart!"

He dug into a chest pocket and pulled out a blue and white Bic pen with a different logo printed on it. "Pen from the competition . . . I won't give it to you, there's no point because they'll be taking everything away from you at the station anyhow."

"The company's looking to get outside customers that way?"

"Bah—no idea. It's advertising . . . Wait, I've got another one . . . The point is to advertise. That's fine with us, seeing how we don't get any more equipment than the police force in like Moldavia or someplace . . ."

I liked this boy's placid way, his indifference to my situation. A plumpish young man the age of Emmanuel, with beardless skin and a shaved scalp. He had big light eyes, slightly reddened. He did me good. I was tempted to drop my head on his shoulder. Through the window, I tried to make out the door of the building. The angle was bad and the streetlight made it hard. I looked up, toward our apartment. There was still a light on in the Manoscrivi place. In our flat everything was dark, but I couldn't see the bedroom window, it looks out the other side. I thought about the cat slapped down somewhere in there, and wondered where I should put the useless glasses lined up on the buffet. How to explain that insanity with the glasses? Once I'd calmed down about enough chairs I'd felt compelled to run through Deuil-l'Alouette and take the bus to the discount store to buy five packs of wine-glasses, two of them large size, specifically for Burgundy reds, plus two boxes of champagne flutes when I already had the Elegance flutes in the house. The glasses waiting on a silly little tablecloth, those glasses made for multiple uses as if we spent our time with people who were sticklers on matters of etiquette and whom my acquired bourgeois standards demanded that I satisfy, those glasses that would never find any space in any cabinet, not to mention all the ones that would be coming out of the dishwasher—those glasses assailed me, coagulated into a monstrous image and formed a mass of anguish. It was, I thought as I scanned the busy parking lot, that insanity of worry and anticipation that attacks the elderly. Getting stressed out by a hypothetical problem. My mother used to take out her bus ticket two blocks before she got to the stop. She would walk with the ticket held out in front of her, pinched in the fingers of her woolen glove. Same thing for her money on any line in a shop. It could happen to me, doing that. Got to prepare for all eventualities, map the terrain. When my mother went to spend a few days with her cousin in Achères (a direct ride from

Asnières) the suitcase was already on the floor, open and carpeted with a few items a week ahead. I do that too, on a scarcely more sensible schedule. Two cars arrived at almost the same time. Some men got out. A sort of cluster formed around the door. I said, "Who are they?"

"The criminal justice officer and the PTS."

"The PTS?"

"The forensics police."

The cluster came apart. Two uniformed officers headed over toward us. The others went into the building. The guys in jeans and leather jackets came right back out, they hurried toward the unmarked car. I caught a glimpse of Jean-Lino, smaller than the rest of them, in his Zara jacket and his pleated trousers. The doors slammed and the car took off with the lights and the noise.

Those clusters come together, come apart. You could describe men's life like that. We too set out in the Police Emergency car. In the shopwindows I saw us passing with the flashing light and the siren howling. There's a certain unreality to seeing yourself being transported at top speed, like seeing your own speeding train reflected in another one. At the station house, I was taken downstairs to a mezzanine. I was set on an iron bench that had handcuffs welded to it. Now I had only a single hand attached. I waited awhile there and then they took me into an office, they told me I had the right to remain silent, to see a doctor, a lawyer, to alert my family. I asked them to call Pierre. I said I had no lawyer and that they could call whoever they wanted. A woman searched me again and took a scraping from the inside of my mouth. In the corridor she asked if I wanted to go to the toilet before I was put into jail (jail!!). The primitive stand-up Turkish latrines. I said to myself, A few hours ago you were slicing an orange cake in your flowing party dress. I went into the dilapidated cell with a bench at the rear. There was a mattress on a linoleum floor with an orange wool blanket folded on it. The woman told me I could rest a little while I waited for the lawyer, who'd be coming at around seven o'clock. She closed the door with an extravagant racket of locks and latches. The wall that gave onto the corridor, including the door, was entirely glass with bars. I sat down on the bench. Was Jean-Lino somewhere in the place? And poor Lydie in her suitcase ... with her scarf on crooked and the crazy hair, the rumpled skirt ... All those ornaments turned useless from one minute to the next. The red Gigi Dool pumps tossed into the grave. A colleague of Pierre's died a month ago. Etienne had phoned to tell Pierre but he got me instead. He asks, "You know who Max Botezarlu is?" "By name." "He just died, instantly, a stroke in the Metro." "A good death," I said. "Oh really—you'd like that kind of death for yourself, would you?" "Yes." "You wouldn't want to see it coming, prepare yourself, like in La Fontaine, *Feeling death was coming he brought together all his dear ones?*" "No. I'm afraid of the deterioration." There was a silence at the other end of the line and then he said, "Still, it's better to die with people around you. Or actually maybe not." I put the orange blanket over my knees. It scratched. I pulled together the edges of Lydie's coat as a liner.

Well then . . . " In the storage room where I meet with the lawyer everything is gray. The floor tiles, the walls, the table, the chairs. Everything. The two chairs are bolted to the floor and so is the table. No openings. Hideous lighting. Earlier I'd had a small carton of orange juice and a dry cracker. Gilles Terneu, lawyer. He had long pepper-and-salt hair brushed back, and a neatly barbered mustache-beard arrangement. A well-groomed man, my mother would have said, who banked on his coiffure from the moment he woke up. I was slightly embarrassed by my Kitty pants and fur slippers, but mostly by the coat that only reached to my forearms. He opened his briefcase, pulled out a notepad and a pen. He said, "Well then . . . Madam, do you know why you're here?" I might be exhausted, but still I knew why I was here. I recounted the events. Well, I mean, the minimal official version.

"What exactly are your ties to this man, madam?"

"He's a friend."

"Madam, you do know that we have a criminal matter here. The investigations to be carried out will be very thorough. Into your life as well. Do not think that at this stage you can conceal things. They'll come out sooner or later."

"He's a friend."

"A friend."

"He's a neighbor who's become a friend."

"Did you suspect anything?"

"What do you mean?"

"When you were watching through the peephole."

"When my husband suggested he should call the police, I'd felt he was hesitant . . ."

"You weren't sure he'd call the police . . ."

"No, I wasn't completely sure he would call the police . . . And when I saw the elevator going down . . . and since I hadn't seen anything or heard anything outdoors, when I was also looking out the window . . ."

"You were in your nightclothes?"

"Yes."

"And your husband? He didn't hear you go down?"

"My husband was sleeping."

"Is he still sleeping?"

"I don't know. I asked them to let him know."

"Does your husband have his doubts about your relationship with this man?"

"No. No, no."

"We don't have much time, ma'am. We have a half

hour and you're going to be—when you leave this inter-view—you'll be questioned by the police, probably even confronted with your neighbor, Monsieur . . ."

"Manoscrivi."

"Manoscrivi. Obviously, one hopes that the two ver-sions do not contradict . . . Do you think he might say something different?"

"No . . . There's no reason to."

"Good. The advice a lawyer gives, as a general rule, is to say as little as possible to the police so as not to be caught up later in one's own statements. Still, your version seems plausible, it's possible that you will have some interest in speaking. That is, in going into some detail. But, madam, I call your attention to the fact that what you say here will later be used as an initial statement of truth to con-test what you say later."

"It is the truth . . . There is one thing I haven't men-tioned . . . which changes nothing but I want to tell everything . . . Actually there are two things . . . Down-stairs, when I was downstairs in the lobby trying to persuade him to call the police, we ran into a neighbor . . ."

"Someone you know?"

"Yes, a girl I say hello and goodbye to—she's the daughter of—"

"Wasn't she surprised to see you at three in the morning?"

"She said hello, she looked as if she was coming in from a party . . ."

"The tenants in the building know you and he are friends?"

"I couldn't say. Yes probably."

"Did she look surprised?"

"No, no, not at all."

"The situation was fairly ordinary . . ."

"Ordinary. She seemed eager to get out of the rain, she went right into the elevator, the whole thing took two seconds. We just crossed paths . . . And the other thing is, after calling the police, Jean-Lino Manoscrivi wanted to put his cat someplace safe. So we went back to his apartment, picked up his cat, and put it in our apartment. His cat is in our place now."

"You seem to be awfully concerned with this man's life . . ."

"Yes . . ."

"And you say that the relationship is only one of friendship."

"Yes."

"You don't think you might have left some trace of a relationship that could seem different in nature from what you describe?"

"No."

"You never exchanged emails, for instance? Your sites will be checked."

"Never any emails."

"And he . . . you don't think he might harbor some feelings . . . you believe you're on the same wavelength?"

"That I can't say, but he's never shown anything . . ."

"There's no material evidence that could imply that this is a romantic relationship even though you declare it a—"

"None."

"For instance, your husband has never been jealous of the relationship?"

"Never."

"You have no reason to help this man in an act that could be a criminal act?"

"None at all."

"You'll be asked the question: You learn your friend has killed his wife . . . How far would you go if he asked you to help him?"

"He didn't ask me to help him."

"If he *had* asked you to . . ."

". . . Help him how?"

"No, ma'am. There you have to say: 'I did not help him, the proof is, I urged him to call the police.' Who called the police? Was it he or you?"

"Both of us."

"What does that mean, both of you? Who was holding the receiver?"

"He was. I dialed 17 and handed him the receiver . . ."

"Ah! You dialed 17."

"Yes."

"If you hadn't run into the neighbor, would you have dialed 17?"

"... Yes ... of course."

"Madam, you must not hesitate on this point."

"Yes, of course."

"It's important."

"Yes, yes."

"Now then. You knew he was in the process of fleeing ..."

"No, I did not know that."

"It was when you went downstairs that ..."

"When I saw the elevator blinking, I called out. I called out, and since I got no answer even though the car was just below my level and I knew I could be heard, I opened the stairwell door. I heard footsteps running down. I know my neighbor takes the stairs and that no one else uses them. I thought something odd was going on. I went down myself, I opened the lobby door and saw him pulling the big suitcase out of the elevator. Then I did understand what was happening ... Because I saw the enormous bulging suitcase ... But as I was going down I had no idea what to expect ..."

"Except that you were expecting the police who didn't arrive."

"Yes ... But it could have been someone else in the elevator ..."

"And so you right away said 'Stop!'"

"Yes. No, I said, 'What are you doing? What's in the suitcase?'"

"Even before you ever saw the young woman neighbor, you'd immediately tried to persuade him not to flee."

"The first thing I did was grab the purse, he was holding a purse and there was a coat lying on top of the suitcase, I took the bag and the coat, I said, 'What are you doing, you're crazy!' And then the neighbor came in . . . that made it easier, the neighbor . . ."

"He told you his wife was in the suitcase? . . ."

"No. I don't recall . . . It was implicit."

"And you had no trouble persuading him . . ."

"I had no trouble, uh . . . No . . . I had no trouble persuading him."

"But if you hadn't been there he would have left?"

"I can't say."

"For him, the neighbor made the difference? If the neighbor hadn't turned up, you wouldn't have managed to persuade him?"

"I can't answer that."

"You don't know."

"No."

"How long have you known him?"

"Three years."

"A relation of friendship."

"Friendship."

"With some intimacy . . . some confidentiality?"

"No . . . We use the formal *vous* with each other."

"He told you about his problems with his wife?"

"No. He didn't have any. I mean I don't think so. He never spoke of any."

"What are your relations with his wife?"

"Very cordial. She came to my party. It was very pleasant."

"You like her?"

"Yes . . ."

"How does it work, in a couple, when a person is friends with one of the two? You're sure there was no . . . You don't think there could have been some jealousy on her part, given the connection between the two of you?"

"He told me a little about what happened after the party and I had nothing to do with . . ."

"Nothing to do with it?"

"Nothing."

"That was the first time you'd invited them over?"

"Yes . . ."

"So, a separate relationship between this man and you, and one not based on . . . intimacy, on confidentiality."

"No."

"Based on what, that relationship?"

"It involved some confidential talk, yes, but about matters in the past . . . Childhood, our respective childhoods, life in general, but we never talked about our marital situations. We'd already spent time together, the four of us. Lydie sang in jazz clubs, it was her hobby, and Jean-Lino took us to listen to her. We all have good memories of it."

"So then: a relationship with nothing hidden about it . . . Madam, I permit myself to insist: Do not play lightly with that. Should it develop that the relationship is not what you describe, there could be problems."

"Our relations are clear."

"Your husband will be questioned. He'll confirm the nature of the connections you've had with this man?"

"Absolutely."

"You're affirmative: you rule out any expression of jealousy on your husband's part? You know very well that a friendship between a man and a woman can—"

"No. No jealousy."

"Excuse me for asking the question, ma'am, but have you ever had any involvement with the penal system before?"

"Never."

"And your husband?"

"No."

"And your neighbor?"

"No. Not that I know of."

"You're sure?"

"For my husband and me, I'm sure."

"And you have complete confidence in that man?"

"Yes."

"What was your reaction when you learned that he had killed: ... You were frightened for him? You were worried for him??"

"Yes."

"But you think that the reasons he had, and that he gave you, can prevail before the law? In the courts? You thought it was best for him to turn himself in?"

"Yes. I think something crazy happened. Maybe the

fact of our party, where everyone did drink a little ... I think that it's a dreadful accident. A fit of madness. He had absolutely no intention of killing his wife."

"So it's best that he should explain himself."

"Certainly."

"Do you envisage for a moment that he'd accuse you of wanting to help him to flee? Or to hide his wife's body?"

"No."

"Madam, from the moment you're seen together, you holding the coat, the handbag, a person could think you're going to help him. Now that's the point that needs to be laid to rest ... He could not accuse you of that?"

"No."

"The young woman, the neighbor—could she accuse you?"

"The neighbor can only say what she saw. I'll confirm that. She saw the two of us in the lobby, he near the door and me behind him holding the coat and the bag."

"Did you speak?"

"No. We heard her coming. We didn't speak. Actually, we were petrified to see her, to be honest. I was petrified because there was a dead body in the suitcase."

"I bet!"

"I was petrified for him and even for me, to tell the truth. I mean, after all, I was aware of being in a situation I should not have been in. Since the suitcase belongs to us."

"The suitcase belongs to you?"

"Yes. I'd lent it to Lydie a few days ago. She wanted to move some things into her office."

"They don't have a suitcase, your neighbors?"

"She wanted to move some linens and cushions that take up a lot of room. And besides, a big suitcase would spare her making a second trip."

"And your neighbor—was he aware of the loan?"

"I don't know. He must have seen it in his house."

"I remind you that what you're going to tell the police soon will be on formal record and will bind you for the future. Everything depends on your good faith and on your ability to convince. Your history holds together. It has the weight of truth. But I call your attention to the fact that the investigations will all be wide-ranging and thorough, your home will be searched, your husband interrogated . . . What is your work, madam?"

"I'm a patent engineer at the Pasteur Institute."

"Did the people at your party witness anything? Any strain between the couple? They will certainly all be questioned."

"I don't know . . . I myself did witness something but I don't know if I should mention it . . . I don't know what he will want to say . . ."

"Careful here, madam, because if you give any impression of not cooperating and excluding some things in order to protect him, you move into an area . . ."

"Well at one point, the conversation turned to a matter that she took very seriously—I tell you this, Counselor, even though it could seem silly—the conversation was about free-range chickens. He made fun of her because she'd asked a waiter in a restaurant if the chicken they serve was allowed to roost—that is, if it had lived a normal life, that kind of thing . . . He was trying to make the rest of us laugh with this story, and after that you felt a kind of chill between them."

"You're supposing that the conflict began over that."

"It's possible . . . She scolded him, when they got upstairs, for humiliating her in company. The argument got poisonous, and at a certain moment—I can't explain, he'd do it better than I can—she gave the cat a kick . . . He grabbed her, he squeezed—"

"You're telling me that they quarreled when she stood up for animal welfare, and he killed her because she kicked the cat."

"I think the animals weren't the point. I mean, they weren't basically in opposition on . . . When a couple quarrels, opinions often serve as an excuse . . . I don't believe she meant to harm the cat. He meant to hurt her, not kill her. Maybe she died of a heart attack. He's not a criminal, he's a very gentle man."

"It's not in your interest to advocate for him."

"I'm only saying it to you."

"All right, but it's not smart to take up his cause. You have a neighborly connection that turned into a friendly connection. You go to his aid to keep him from fleeing his responsibilities because you think that would be worse.

Period. You must understand that what you're suspected of is complicity and concealing a body."

"What do I risk?"

"You've never been convicted. You have a profession. Everything depends on what he says. Your husband has been notified?"

"Supposedly, yes."

"What is he going to say? . . . When you two went up there, why didn't you demand that he call the police right away?"

"We did demand it. Well, my husband did."

"And you went back down to your flat even though he hadn't called?"

"He said he wanted to be alone, that he needed a little time. My husband, suddenly, decided that we had no business there, that we'd done our duty and that it wasn't up to us to call the police. And we went downstairs."

"By the way, what was the reason Monsieur Manoscrivi came down to your place after killing his wife?"

"I think he couldn't stay alone . . ."

"Do your colleagues at work know of his existence?"

"No."

"At your party your behavior wouldn't have given the least—"

"No."

"The young woman neighbor couldn't say there was anything ambiguous about your behavior . . . Were you far apart from each other when she saw you?"

"Yes. I mean, a normal distance."

"...The police suspicion may consist in this: that it's the neighbor's arrival that forced you to notify the police, and that that was not your original intention. How do you counter that?"

"What would I have been doing there in slippers and pajamas, with nothing . . . ?"

"How much time elapsed between when you were downstairs and when you notified the police?"

"A half hour . . . Not even. The time it took to convince him to go up to get the cat and put it in our apartment."

"Still, it's the neighbor's presence that led him to agree to turn himself in."

"I can't say otherwise."

"Did you often go to his apartment?"

"Almost never. Maybe once. Today yes—that is, yesterday, I went up with Lydie, to get some chairs. She was lending me chairs for the party."

"Good. You'll undergo questioning. Which won't necessarily be easy, it's possible they'll play on your nerves a little and that two people will question you at the same time, because there may be a suspicion of complicity not in the criminal act but in the aftermath. That you tried to conceal the body, and so on. So be careful during that segment. What you say will matter. I don't see them holding you for more than twenty-four hours. If Monsieur Manoscrivi corroborates your version and if your husband gives no information that . . . he says nothing that might lead to any confusion, you'll be out by this evening."

I did leave in the early evening. Pierre came to get me. He had been questioned during the afternoon. I handed over the long coat. I was free. In all likelihood, Jean-Lino confirmed that he acted alone. Now he had disappeared, dragged down some dark hole. In the car Pierre was sullen. Instead of comforting me. He looked tired and sad. He told me that he didn't like this whole business. I said I don't see how anyone could possibly like it. He asked me what I had actually done.

"I did what I said I did. Nobody can understand how you managed to go to sleep," I said.

"I'd had too much to drink. I was done in."

"You didn't mention the bathroom?"

"You really think I'm some jackass."

"I was afraid you would, to keep me in the clear . . ."

"You helped him?!"

"No!"

"Explain to me about the suitcase. Really explain it."

"I lent Lydie the suitcase to move some stuff to her office."

"When?"

"I don't know . . . A couple of days ago."

"So he sees a suitcase in his house, he says to himself, Ah, good size, I'll put my wife inside."

"I couldn't foresee that."

"My Delsey suitcase!! Shit!"

"I'm sorry . . ."

"And nice job with the cat. I nearly had a heart attack. There would have been two corpses last night."

A little before the police phoned him, he had got up to look for me around the apartment. In the entryway he'd stepped on something soft. It was Eduardo's tail, sticking out from beneath a chest. The beast had let loose a strident howl. Terrified, Pierre had pressed the light switch and discovered the cat, muzzle flat to the floor, the rest of his body pulled back under the chest, staring at him with terrified eyes. When we got home to the parking lot, I raised my head. I looked up at the building. At our floor, at the one above. I thought, There's nobody at all up there. The mimosa branches waved gently. I said, "Who's going to take care of the plants?"

"What plants?"

"Lydie's plants."

"Nobody. The apartment is sealed."

I was stunned. The mimosa, the crocuses, the buds, all that new life I'd seen the day before in the array of unmatched pots. And I saw her again, leaning into her little patch of garden, taking the inexpressibly white crocus between her fingers to hand it to me. We got out of the car. I saw the Laguna still parked in the same spot. The lobby was empty. As impersonal as ever. We took the elevator. Our apartment was impeccable. Pierre had cleaned the kitchen. He'd cleared a space for the litter box and the table was set for two. I had not expected that kindness. It was all I needed to start me crying.

I don't know how many times I was interrogated after that. The detectives from the police headquarters, the ones from the crime squad, some kind of personality investigator (he used some other title but I've forgotten it; I didn't understand if he was investigating my personality or Jean-Lino's), the examining magistrate. As to the sequence of events, always more or less the same questions. With a few variants: Why did we offer the suspect a cognac instead of going to help his wife? Had we touched the body? (Fortunately I had put the scarf on her, I also said I'd touched her legs while Pierre took her pulse.) The magistrate, whom I liked, asked me—in these terms—how it happened that my husband saw fit to go off to bed, when he had just discovered his neighbor's dead body? And of course the question the lawyer had asked kept coming back in various forms: What would you have done if the third party had not arrived on the scene? But the terrain that lawyer Gilles Terneu had not explored, and which everyone tried ad nauseam to get me to take on, was the terrain of my life. What was she all about, this Elisabeth Jauze, née Rainguez in Puteaux? That's called The Full Identity, it seems, in police language. Everything you ever carefully buried must be brought back to life. Everything you've crossed out you must write again, in tidy lettering. Childhood, parents, youth, school, good choices and bad. They examined my life with ridiculous zeal. That was my impression—a ridiculous determination to manufacture a false picture. A little sociology packet they'll put into the dossier and that will say nothing. The justice system will have done its job. For me, it brought back images I was unaware had stayed around somewhere—the bar in Dieppe, the big dormant limo decorated for the carnival and set going again in the fog—I didn't know I was still carrying them with me. You can't understand who people are outside the landscape. The landscape is crucial. It's the landscape that is the true filiation. The room and the stone as much as the segment of sky. That's what Denner taught me to see in the pictures they call "street photography": how the landscape illuminates the man. And how, in return, it is part of him. And I can say that this is what I've always liked about Jean-Lino—the way he carried the landscape inside him, without guarding against anything.

The next day, I went to the Pasteur as if everything were normal. I had lunch in the canteen with Danielle. On the telephone all we'd said was that we had things to tell. We found a table near a window, set down our trays, I said, "Who goes first?"

"Go ahead, you go."

"You won't be disappointed."

She was all ears. "You remember that couple who were there Saturday night, a woman with an orange-dyed mane and her husband?"

"Yes, your neighbors."

"Our neighbors. He strangled her that night."

"She's dead?"

"Well, yes."

Anyone else would have put on a horrified look. Not my Danielle—she lit up. "No?!"

She had no idea of my relation with Jean-Lino. I gave her an account of the night (the official one, need I specify). A very lively report. Urged on by her beneficent frivolity, I took care with all the effects: the doorbell, the cat, the suitcase, the lobby, the cops, the jail cell . . . From time to time, Danielle would say "It's insane!!" or some such remark. She was enchanted.

"And what will you do with the cat?"

"I don't know. I haven't an atom of feeling for him."

"We could give him to my mother."

"Your mother? . . ."

"She lives in a ground-floor in Sucy. There's a little square of lawn in front, he'd be very happy."

"But what about her?"

"That will pull her out of her funk over Jean-Pierre. She adores cats, she's had them before."

"Ask her about it."

"I'll call her tonight."

"And what about you? . . . While this was going on . . . Mathieu Crosse?"

I had no sooner finished saying Mathieu Crosse than a yoke of depression fell onto my shoulders. Here we were trading story for story as we started on the lemon tart, the insane neighbor stacked against the potential lover: Jean-Lino, do excuse me. But Danielle is subtle. Rather than describe her Saturday night, with that faculty we women have for thickening the slimmest amorous anecdote, conferring weight on no matter what word or insignificant detail, she set about understating the significance of her encounter. Something that might have given us joy and the thread of an unending tale became a small tale verging on sad. She had driven Mathieu Crosse home in her car. Double-parked in front of his house. He had the delicacy (in view, she assumed, of her newly bereaved situation) not to suggest that she come upstairs. Touched by this thoughtfulness, and after a few awkward clinches in the front seat, she parked properly.

He'd had to confess that he was boarding his sixteen-year-old son for the weekend. The boy was out but could be back at any moment. Ultimately, they did slip into the apartment like a couple of thieves afraid of getting caught. Toward four o'clock in the morning, ejected upon the son's arrival, she went home in something of a whirl. "You like him?" I asked.

"I don't know."

"Liar."

"I kinda do."

I told her that she would be interrogated as a witness, as would Mathieu and all my guests, by the crime squad. She was far from unhappy at the prospect.

⌐

Only Georges Verbot showed no surprise when we told people. The woman was asking to get hit with a pickax, he said. Claudette El Ouardi emerged from her reserve to say that she had noticed something wasn't quite right with that Manoscrivi fellow.

She had noticed it when they met at the front door and he'd introduced himself by way of some incomprehensible sally. Later on she'd felt embarrassed at the sight of his euphoria over Gil Teyo-Diaz needling Mimi. His imitation of the chicken beating its wings had upset her, as much for the vulgarity of the act as for his views. While never imagining such an abominable development, she had sensed madness around his antics. All her comments, proffered over the phone in her even tones, showed me how much closer I was to a Jean-Lino than to a Claudette, whose stiffness I'd hitherto attributed to a form of scientist's introversion but now suddenly saw as revealing a shameful conformism. Before she grew into a great stringbean and lost her vocation, my sister Jeanne used to dance. Our parents and I went to see her perform in a year-end gala. She did a little solo at stage-front that everyone applauded. There were drinks afterward in the cafeteria of the Maison des Jeunes. Our parents were mingling with the others, who complimented them on Jeanne. My father wasn't accustomed to that sort of thing. He thought he'd get through it by joking. People smiled politely. It was clear to me that the jokes were going a little off the mark but he got excited without realizing anything. At a certain point he chuckled, his nostrils reddened and dilated, and said, "Yeah she's great, pretty soon we could send her out into the street to dance and pass the hat." People turned away and the four of us were left alone. Another time, my high-school music teacher organized a trip to the Olympia music hall to see Michel Polnareff. My father drove us in from Puteaux with two classmates and their mother. In the Sani-Chauffe company van, which was actually our usual car, he said, "Somebody's gotta explain to me why the national school system would send you kids to see that faggot!" When my classmates reached adolescence and he'd run into one of them at the house, he would pat her behind or grip a breast and exclaim, "Oh it's coming along nice now, you're turning into a big girl, Caroline honey!" The girl would laugh convulsively and I'd say "Papa please!!" He'd laugh, "What, I'm just checking out the goods, no harm in that!" These days he'd go straight to jail. My father made me ashamed, often, but I was never able to cross to the other side. No character on a plain background ever interested me. Except to Danielle, then Emmanuel and Bernard, we gave no details on the business here. I told nobody about my involvement, nor about my session at the police station. Not even Jeanne, who anyhow was all tied up in her erotic passion. Catherine Mussin was the only one who said *the poor thing* about Lydie. The others considered the event abstractly horrible and were curious about the details and the why. I must confess to feeling a certain delectation in announcing the thing. It's not unpleasant to be the bearer of sensational news. But I should have stopped there. Managed to hang up right away, and not be drawn into any chatter. There's no purity in the human relationship. *The poor thing.* I ask myself whether the term applies. We can't judge only living persons by the criteria of our situation. It's absurd to pity a dead person. But you can complain of destiny. The mixture of suffering and a probable inanity. Yes. In that sense *the poor thing* does apply. I can say *the poor things* about my father, about my mother, Joseph Denner, the Savannah couple, the Jehovah's Witness in front of the enormous wall, some dead people from my black-and-white photography books, those folks in the tomb portraits in San Michele, dressed up like kings among their fake flowers but whose lives we sense were not always rosy, the numberless obscurities from before, all the people whose deaths the newspapers bundle together into utter meaninglessness. I think of that line of Jankélévitch's about his father: "What was the point of that little stroll [he had to take] through the firmament of destiny? ..." Ought we to say "poor thing" about Lydie Gumbiner? In her highly colored world, Lydie Gumbiner had wafted above any vicissitudes. I can only think of her in movement, I see her crossing the parking lot, her skirts fluttering, like a lively little woman in a George Grosz drawing, or patting the cleavage of her bosom beneath a tumble of hair. On her leaflet she had written, "The voice and the rhythm matter more than the words and the meaning." Lydie Gumbiner had sung, militated, spun her crystal pendant: in her way she had dodged Nothingness.

—⁓

Danielle's mother agreed to take Eduardo. We arranged to bring him to her at Sucy-en-Brie the next Sunday. Meanwhile, I had settled something that was bothering me. After careful examination of the front of our apartment building, I went up to see the sixth-floor tenant, Monsieur Aparicio, a retiree from the Postal Service, not much of a talker.

As I passed the door of the Manoscrivis, I saw the wax seals and the yellow notice form where the line "Infraction" was filled out: "Intentional Homicide." Monsieur Aparicio is mostly bald but the remaining hair at the back of his head is caught in a little bow. A touch of modernity that gave me courage. I told him my plan, which was to hook up a hose with a pistol nozzle in his apartment so that the Manoscrivi plants could be watered from above, from his balcony. "I'm not asking you to do it, Monsieur Aparicio," I said. "I'll come myself to take care of it, if you allow me, twice a week, at whatever time might suit you, early morning or evening." Several minutes later, and after hearing my long-winded plea, he let me come in. We went into the living room, he opened the window. We leaned out over the parapet, I said, "You see how pretty it is, all their plantings. The rain can't get to even the mimosa." On his own balcony there was a bicycle, a table, and some tools. As to greenery, a couple of vaguely soil-filled pots and an old fern. Where would the hose be hooked up? he asked. In the kitchen, I said.

"Gotta get at least a twenty-yarder."

"Yes, of course!! Thank you, Monsieur Aparicio!"

He never offered me a coffee, and our exchanges remained limited to meteorologic matters. I am doubly grateful to him. First, for never having fussed about the drama itself (including the day when the police extended the investigation to all the neighbors), and second, for not taking over my role as irrigator. I bought an excellent expandable hose with a universal hookup and a variable nozzle that made it possible to water from a distance. Aparicio himself attaches it to his faucet and starts the flow before I arrive each time. He could do the job at any hour he chose and free himself from the servitude of our appointments. He must have sensed the fetishism that binds me to this task and has always respected it. Since his eviction to our flat, Eduardo had immured himself in a state of hostile moroseness. He would wander from one piece of furniture to another, crouching underneath them or clinging to the shadowy corners. He did agree to eat, and Pierre managed to get the last Revigot 200 pills into him, crushed in some tuna-fish mash. On my return to the apartment, the night before our excursion to Sucy, I witnessed the following scene: The fishing pole was twitching from inside the bathroom, and in the corridor Eduardo kept a dull eye on the caprices of the leopard tail.

At the sight of me he fled, while Pierre, seated naked on the toilet, focused on his magnetic chessboard and its manual, went on waving the pole with one hand. In Deuil-l'Alouette, there's a Raminogrobis shop that does cats and dogs. To carry Eduardo to Danielle's mother, I bought a travel container in hard plastic. I took the mid-range one at thirty-nine euros so he'd be more comfortable. In the front hall, everything stood ready: Jean-Lino's canvas bag and all the accessories, including the T-shirt, the litter box, and the brand-new cage with its grille door open, awaiting only its occupant. The minute he saw it, Eduardo detested the travel cage. He tried to flee, but Pierre grabbed him, shouting "Close the doors!" He positioned the cat at the opening and tried to keep him there. We pushed, the cat resisted, his front paws rigid and overextended, he slipped a little on the floor, the cage slid away at the same time. We tried to persuade him by talking to him, I even think we managed a few Italian-style words. Eduardo tried every means to escape, squirming and biting Pierre's arms as Pierre yelled at me. Once or twice he lost hold and we had to start over. We put toys into the case, the Feliway diffuser, some fish patties. The cat would have none of it. After twenty minutes of exhausting battle, Pierre thought of standing the cage on end, with the open door on top. Pouring with sweat, in a fury, he caught Eduardo and dropped him in vertically, headfirst through the opening. There was a weird moment when I saw that the head and the front paws were inside. Pierre was holding the cage, he said, "Help him in, help him!" I shoved him down as best I could with my eyes closed. We slammed the gate shut. The cage was strewn with smashed fish patties. Eduardo howled, but he was howling from inside.

The aunt didn't recognize me. She was seated beside her walker, with a bib around her neck, in a windowless annex cafeteria, alone before a plate of fish and mashed potatoes. I hadn't expected her to be at dinner at six o'clock. It's a great effort for me to adjust to that terrifying schedule. I see it as a means of disposing of people. The only people you can cause to eat dinner at that hour are the vulnerable ones you want to unload into bed (at hostels people are already there). I introduced myself, said I had come once before with Jean-Lino. She looked me over carefully. There's sometimes a certain icy authority in the gaze of the old. Her name was Benilde. I learned that at the front desk—Benilde Poggio—but I didn't dare pronounce it. The receptionist had said, "Oh the lady from the Dolomites!" I know the Dolomites from Dino Buzzati books. Denner was reading "Mountains of Glass": portraits of alpinists, laments for the destruction of nature, for the slopes the writer would never walk again. It was so to speak Denner's bedside book. He used to read me chapters aloud. Some of them were masterpieces. I remembered one piece on the conquest of Everest: "In the old fortress, atop the highest tower, there was still one small room where no one had ever gone. The door was finally opened. Man entered in, and he saw. There is no mystery left." The woman from the Dolomites has long hands that are thick and a little callused. The fingers all move together as if they were glued. With her fork she deboned the fish, which was already deboned. I asked if I was disturbing her; I said, You may want to dine quietly? She made a kind of carpet of the potatoes which she then brought to her mouth. I thought her head shook less than the last time. She watched me as she chewed. Occasionally she lifted the bib to her lips. I thought the hairdresser had overdone the mauve tinting. And the curl too. They must have a coiffeur in the home.

I no longer understood what I was doing there. What is the point of this fantasy of benevolence that consists of visiting a woman who's a stranger to you and who doesn't even know who you are? She was wearing a long sweater with pockets. She felt around in one of them and pulled out a little plastic packet tied with a string and held it out to me. In an unknown language, she told me to smell it. It smelled of cumin. Is that cumin? I asked. *Sì, cumino.* She wanted me to sniff again. I said I liked cumin a lot. And coriander, too. She gestured that I should open the packet. The knot was fairly tight and she couldn't manage with her swollen fingers. When I opened it she signaled me to pour a bit of cumin into the hollow of her hand. By means of trembling movements she indicated that it need be only a pinch. She had me smell the grains again in her hand and, laughing, she scattered them onto the fish. I laughed too. She said something I didn't understand completely but in passing I caught Lydie's name. And I thought I understood that it was Lydie who had given her the packet. I'd never made the connection between the aunt and Lydie. How stupid of me. She was Jean-Lino's wife, how could she not have known the aunt? She set before me, with the spoon, the lemon yogurt from her tray. We could hear sounds of voices in the corridor, sounds of doors, of things rolling. Without knowing how, one knew these were the sounds of evening—contained sounds, that would not be heard anywhere else. I thought of the visit I'd made with Jean-Lino, when she had talked about her chickens coming into the house and settling everywhere. This time the aunt spoke neither of chickens nor of cowbells. She had taken on other habits far from mountain life, a thousand leagues from the great shadows that swell and shrink. She had got used to the smooth walls and the wooden railings, she had agreed to watch time melt away no matter where.

⁓

Buzzati saw the immobility of mountains as their prime attribute. "The reason, I believe, is that man seeks a state of absolute tranquility," he wrote. Etienne Dienesmann hiked with his children on the trails he'd walked in the past with his father. They picnicked at the foot of the same cliffs. They raised their eyes to the same array of peaks. With the father gone, everything was still in place in the limpid chill. Every summer, surrounded by laughter, he felt his own unimportance. Eventually he came to experience it without bitterness.

⁓

Dear Jean-Lino,
   Before I ask you to listen to my elucubrations on the fate of objects, you should know that in Sucy-en-Brie at

Danielle's mother's house (you met Danielle, the documentation manager who'd just come from her stepfather's burial) Eduardo seems to have become nice. That's the word that was used. Do animals change their nature? I would sooner attribute it to the helpful adjustment of two creatures in mourning. I know you were worried about him and we've kept you informed of his transfer. According to the latest reports, he spends his days on the sill of a ground-floor window, like the old folks in the villages of the South who watch life go by from their doorstep. He oversees the dirt plot where real birds and real mice frolic in full safety for, contrary to the fears of his new owner, he never leaves his post. If not exactly proud of him, at least be easy about him. My mother died last month. In a shoebox in her house I found the nutcracker I made in eighth grade. For one experimental year, girls were given access to the iron- and woodworking shops in the boys' school. None of us chose metalworking, but a few of us plunged into wood-working to avoid sewing class. The teacher was a Chinese man with a wig, a madman. We would finish up fifteen minutes early to leave time for putting the tools back. If the hand plane protruded so much as two millimeters beyond its compartment in the rack, he would scream and slap the kids. Almost the whole year was spent making a nut-cracker. The boys built a model with two levels, a kind of press; the girls a mushroom-shaped model. Mine was two colors with a hat that looked like an acorn painted dark brown. When I gave it to my father, I put some walnuts in the package. At first, seeing the object, he exclaimed, "It's a cock, your thing here!" And then he was impressed when he saw that it worked. My father loved tools and respected the worker. He showed the nutcracker to everyone—that is, to his sister Micheline and friends, to one or two colleagues who came by for a drink at the house from time to time. He wanted to know how I'd made the thread of the screw section, if I'd used a special gouge. He'd say "Pass me Elisabeth's cock" and do a demonstration with everything that had a shell. He'd say "smooth turn, quiet cracking, impeccable walnut." It didn't bother me that he'd say cock, it even made me laugh. That all went on for a while, until everyone forgot about the nutcracker. It must have stayed in the kitchen on a fruit plate and then it disappeared. I never would have thought it went on existing somewhere. I didn't even remember it. Now it's lying right in front of me, alongside a newer pepper grinder. It looks astoundingly comfortable. Why do certain objects fall apart and others not? When we emptied my mother's apartment, if it had been my sister who opened the shoebox she would have tossed it out without a thought along with the other old stuff. Lydie believed in the destiny of things. Would it be so impossible, after all, that the rose quartz in her pendant really had been a gift to her? (I should tell you by the way that I'm not so far myself from asking in restaurants, and also at the butcher's—where I go less and less—if the chickens were free to fly around, the pigs to wallow, just as I can no longer stand to see an animal on display as an attraction since I started getting the bulletins from her organization.) Jean-Lino, even with the judge's green light, you and I have only exchanged notes that are short, and from my side hideously stiff, despite my intentions to the contrary. None of my letters, though they're spurred by an authentic impulse to write, has ever left my house, and none ever really took off. So far it's been impossible for me to find the right tone. This one too I began by thinking I wouldn't send either. So I'm speaking to you freely, as we always did, without worrying about the imbalance of condition between us, or about your state of mind. I can just as easily go on about a nutcracker as confess to you for instance that in the early days of my return (my return!) I had to battle a sense of abandonment and the depression that comes when a period of time draws to an end and closes over. No more Manoscrivis above our heads. The Manoscrivis on the fifth floor were the familiar order of things. I know how laughable that can seem compared to the news of the world, but what disappeared with you is an invisible good, the kind we never think about, it's life we take for granted.

~

We went out on the balcony to watch the arrival of the police van and the squad cars.

Truth to tell, half the building was at their windows.

I leaned out and looked up. Aparicio was there too. He pulled back instantly, uncomfortable at being seen. The reenactment was scheduled for eleven at night. The nighttime hour was meant to replicate the original conditions. We were also told that we should wear the same clothing we had on at the time of the events. I laid out the undershorts and the Kitty pajamas on the bed, like costumes for a play. A dozen people came into the building, one of them a woman carrying a case and a small folding table. Jean-Lino stepped out of the van between two uniformed cops, his hands cuffed. Seeing him, from up there in the Zara biker jacket and the hat from the racetrack, threw me for a loop. I felt as if there'd been some gigantic mistake. From the standpoint of death and the universe, as I suddenly seemed to see things from my parapet, all this insane activity around an inoffensive man—bound and redisguised as himself—struck my eyes as a grotesque farce.

The examining magistrate wanted to start with what he termed "the exit from the party." For that first segment, he thought it unnecessary to dress up as we were three months ago. The stenographer was seated on the landing, at her folding table, before a little portable computer. Photo number one, said the judge: *Policewoman playing the role of Madame Gumbiner.* A tiny woman with curly hair posed, with her arms glued to her sides, in an oversized basque vest. Jean-Lino, looking just as much a stuffed figure, stood by the elevator in a violet shirt and shorter hair. He was uncuffed. He looked younger, I thought. New variable-lens glasses in metal frames freshened him up. The door to the service stairs stood open. One group of officers was stationed in the stairwell. On the landing I recognized the chief investigator from the Paris criminal police, and one of the cops from the lobby during the arrest. The judge wanted to know in what order people had left our apartment. None of the three of us could recall. After a slight muddle, it was vaguely settled that Lydie was the first to cross the threshold, after the El Ouardis, who were not deemed worth representing. The judge posed the new Manoscrivi couple together with Pierre and me in our doorway for the photo: *Madame Gumbiner and Monsieur Manoscrivi leave the Jauze apartment—with Monsieur and Madame El Ouardi who take the elevator.* The judge stressed the importance of the narration in talking to me: The photo file will be distributed at the time of the trial, he said, it is an instructional tool for the president of the court. Later, when he orders a photo of *Monsieur Jauze returning to his bedroom to go to sleep,* he will tell me, "It is important for the jury members to understand that you were left alone." After this preamble, they all walked up to the next floor. Pierre and I went into our living room. Pierre asked me in a hateful tone if I wanted to watch a little of the news while we waited. I had no desire to see the news. He took his chessboard and sat down to study a problem. He hated it all, and particularly his recruitment into each new episode of the business. When we received the summons for the reenactment, he'd sworn to high heaven that he would not be part of it. Sitting now with nothing to do on the couch next to my husband, I observed the apartment as it had never been in normal times. The cushions equidistant and plumped up, the random mounds of things moved into tidy bookish piles. The gleaming floor, with nothing lying about. My mother would have arranged it all this way. The finger on the trouser seam before the authority of the law. We could hear footsteps and the sound of voices upstairs. I said, "Is he going to strangle the policewoman?"

"Let's hope not."

I stretched out, laying my head on his legs. That put him in a very uncomfortable position. I said, "Will he put her into the suitcase?"

"Not before he comes down here to us."

He set the magnetic chessboard on my breasts and the press-clipping account of a game over my face. On the landing, Jean-Lino had behaved like a stranger—mechanical body, fleeting glance. It seemed as if all ties had come undone, including those with the walls of the building. I had not expected that coldness. In the worst years, during preadolescence, I was sent to summer camp in the Vercors mountains. I was always trailing around in those camps where you were left to your own devices and everyone seemed more emancipated and bolder than I was. Sometimes I managed to get myself included by making a few friends. Since we didn't come from the same towns, we'd meet again only the following year. I would look forward to that happily. But I never found the girls the same as they'd been the last time. They were distant, stuck-up, as if we'd never been friends. It affected me all the more because I set so much store by these recovered bonds. I made a sudden movement and a few pawns flew off the chessboard. I went into my bedroom to put on my costume, my Kitty T-shirt and my nicely ironed checkered pajama pants and my fake-fur slippers. I heard Pierre grumbling next door.

Jean-Lino came back and rang our doorbell, with his retinue. Pierre opened the door to him in pale pink boxer shorts. I appeared in my getup. We went into the living room. Jean-Lino took over the Moroccan chair again. Seated higher than us like last time, almost as marmorial, but this time nicely coiffed and without the mouth tic. A good match for our spiffy living room. We opened the brandy. Drained the glasses. The table lamp was turned off, I turned on the ceiling light, turned off the ceiling light, lit the floor lamp. I tidied stuff that was already tidied. I brought out my beloved Rowenta hand vacuum. Pierre took it. He went and attacked Jean-Lino with it. Jean-Lino let it happen undisturbed. The more the judge labored to set the world in order the more things seemed to represent some utter madness. Our little procession moved into the service stairwell in muffled silence. Pierre at the head, with a slowness secretly designed to undercut my collaborationist zeal. The photo was taken at the turn of the stairs, from the Manoscrivi landing above. The seals had been lifted away. We entered the apartment where ten people awaited us in semidarkness. We moved toward the bedroom. Through the open doorway I saw Lydie's feet with the red-strapped pumps. Moving into the room I had a real shock. Lydie below Nina Simone. She had not a hair on her—her face was shapeless and bald. It was a terrifying mannequin, dressed in the paneled flowing skirt and Gigi Dool shoes. Can you show us, the judge said, how you ascertained that Madame Gumbiner was actually dead? Pierre took the pulse. I felt along the legs as I had mentioned in my depositions. The contact was unpleasant, a cold dense foam. I tied a scarf on her, a different one found in the same drawer. As I knotted it the head contracted. Shot number fourteen: *Madame Jauze ties the scarf while Monsieur Manoscrivi closes Madame Gumbiner's mouth.* Jean-Lino went through the motions without the least will to do them well. He seemed to dislike the doll. It was strange to see the chamber pot again, the pewter owl, the crystal pendant, even Nina Simone in her crocheted string dress. They were the PAST. I knew I was seeing them for the last time. Monsieur Jauze, can you show us exactly where you were standing when you urged Monsieur Manoscrivi to call the police? Pierre did a little spin in his miniskirt and his loafers and said, Here.

"What were your last words as you left the apartment?"

"I don't remember now," Pierre said.

"And you, Monsieur Manoscrivi, do you remember?"

"No . . ."

"Madame Jauze? . . . You've said that your husband advised Monsieur Manoscrivi not to wait too long before calling the police."

"Yes. That's right."

"Can you show us how you left Monsieur Manoscrivi?"

Pierre and I went out of the bedroom. At the bathroom the judge stopped us. "You're leaving the room so peacefully? You've said that your husband exerted some pressure to get you to leave the apartment."

"Yes, that's so."

"Can you show us?"

We went back into the bedroom. Pierre gripped my wrist with his steel fingers and pulled me toward the hallway. I let myself be led, leaving Jean-Lino against a backdrop of flowered curtain, standing beside the yellow velvet armchair.

They all wanted to look through the peephole. The judge, the chief investigator, Jean-Lino's lawyer and the public advocate. Each of them, imbued with the required gravity, was fully able to observe that the elevator button could be seen to blink. The lobby was ready for our arrival downstairs. The stenographer was pressed against the wall by the trashcans with the folding table and her PC. The second-floor neighbor was waiting near the windowed entry door, chewing gum. Jean-Lino stood at the elevator. They'd had him put on his hat, his Zara jacket, and his sheepskin gloves. The green coat hung to either side of his folded arm as he clumsily held Lydie's bag by the handle. At the judge's invitation he opened the elevator door and pulled out the suitcase. It looked to me less bulging than with Lydie inside it. The mannequin must have turned out to be more supple, luckily for Jean-Lino, who had had to fold her into the suitcase by himself.

"This is what you saw when you reached the bottom of the stairs?" the judge asked me.

"Yes."

"That's not what you described. On document page DIII, you said that Madame Gumbiner's coat was lying on top of the suitcase . . ."

"Oh, yes. That's possible."

"So where was the coat?"

"On top of the suitcase."

"Do you agree, Monsieur Manoscrivi?"

"Yes."

"Can you show us how the coat was set on top of the suitcase?"

Jean-Lino laid the coat on the suitcase. I confirmed that it was correct thus. The judge entered the datum into the record and ordered the photo. "Monsieur Manoscrivi, can you recall what Madame Jauze said when she saw you?"

"She asked what was in the suitcase."

"And you answered her what?"

"I didn't answer. I went toward the door."

"Can you recall for us how Madame Jauze intercepted you?"

"She grabbed the bag and the coat."

"Madame Jauze, can you show us how you grabbed the bag and the coat?"

I seized the coat, and the bag he was still holding up high with his folded arm. We finally looked at each other. I saw again what I liked in his eyes. Above no matter what sorrow, the flame of mischief. Photo number thirty-two: *Monsieur Manoscrivi watching Elisabeth Jauze take hold of the coat and the bag.*

When the van started up, Jean-Lino pressed his face to the window. They'd put his handcuffs back on. He leaned forward as if to signal me. I was standing outside the windowed front door in my slippers and I waved until the car rounded the building across the way. I stayed there a moment outside when everyone else had gone away. The parking lot was empty. It was a nice starry night in Deuil-l'Alouette. Before it disappeared, the vehicle had made a U-turn between the parked cars to leave in the opposite direction. Jean-Lino was still turned toward me, but what with the darkness and the distance I could no longer make out his face. I could see only the dark shape of his hat, the outmoded accessory that had set him apart and now seemed to toss him back into the anonymous mass of mankind. History was writing itself out above our heads.

We could not hold back what was happening, It was Jean-Lino Manoscrivi who'd just gone by and at the same time it was any man being carried off. I remembered the sense of belonging to some dim whole that Jean-Lino had felt in the Parmentier courtyard when his father used to read the psalm aloud. I looked at the sky and the people there.

Then I climbed back up the service staircase alone.

ABOUT THE AUTHOR

Playwright and novelist Yasmina Reza's work has been translated into more than thirty-five languages. Her play *Art* was the first non-English language play to win a Tony Award, *Conversations After a Burial*, *The Unexpected Man*, and *Life X 3* have all been award-winning critical and commercial successes internationally, and *God of Carnage*, which also won a Tony Award, was adapted for film by Roman Polanski. A new play, *Bella Figura*, premiered in Germany in May 2015. Her fiction includes *Hammerklavier*, *Desolation*, and *Adam Haberberg*. Reza lives in Paris.

ABOUT THE TRANSLATOR

A longtime fiction editor at *The New Yorker* magazine, Linda Asher (translator) has translated Victor Hugo, Balzac, Simenon, Kundera and many other writers. She has been awarded the Scott Moncrieff, the Deems Taylor, the French-American/Florence Gould Translation Prizes, and is a Chevalier of the Order of Arts and Letters of the French Republic.

ABOUT SEVEN STORIES PRESS

Seven Stories Press is an independent book publisher based in New York City. We publish works of the imagination by such writers as Nelson Algren, Russell Banks, Octavia E. Butler, Ani DiFranco, Assia Djebar, Ariel Dorfman, Coco Fusco, Barry Gifford, Martha Long, Luis Negrón, Peter Plate, Hwang Sok-yong, Lee Stringer, and Kurt Vonnegut, to name a few, together with political titles by voices of conscience, including Subhankar Banerjee, the Boston Women's Health Collective, Noam Chomsky, Angela Y. Davis, Human Rights Watch, Derrick Jensen, Ralph Nader, Loretta Napoleoni, Gary Null, Greg Palast, Project Censored, Barbara Seaman, Alice Walker, Gary Webb, and Howard Zinn, among many others. Seven Stories Press believes publishers have a special responsibility to defend free speech and human rights, and to celebrate the gifts of the human imagination, wherever we can. In 2012 we launched Triangle Square books for young readers with strong social justice and narrative components, telling personal stories of courage and commitment. For additional information, visit www.sevenstories.com.